Annie G. Rogers, Ph.D., is a writer, psychoanalyst, and printmaker. She is Analyst of the School at the Lacanian School of Psychoanalysis, where she teaches and supervises. She was a professor for much of her professional life, serving on faculties at Harvard University and Hampshire College. Dr. Rogers has published short fiction and poetry as well as three non-fiction clinical books: *A Shining Affliction: A Story of Harm and Healing in Psychotherapy (1995)*; *The Unsayable: The Hidden Language of Trauma (2005);* and *Incandescent Alphabets: Psychosis and the Enigma of Language (2016)*. Currently, she makes prints and artist's books at Zea Mays Printmaking in Florence, Massachusetts, and is compiling a book of poetry, *Becoming Bird.* She divides her time between Western Massachusetts and Lismore, Ireland.

To Íde B. O'Carroll, who accompanies me into the wilds
of writing every day of my life.

Annie G Rogers

AFTER WORDS

AUSTIN MACAULEY PUBLISHERS™

LONDON • CAMBRIDGE • NEW YORK • SHARJAH

Ordering Information
Quantity sales: Special discounts are available on quantity purchases by corporations, associations, and others. For details, contact the publisher at the address below.

Publisher's Cataloging-in-Publication data
Rogers, Annie G
After Words

ISBN 9781649795717 (Paperback)
ISBN 9798891552876 (ePub e-book)

Library of Congress Control Number: 2024907377

www.austinmacauley.com/us

First Published 2024
Austin Macauley Publishers LLC
40 Wall Street, 33rd Floor, Suite 3302
New York, NY 10005
USA

mail-usa@austinmacauley.com
+1 (646) 5125767

Where do words come from?
from what rubbing of sounds are they born
on what flint do they light their wicks
what winds brought them into our mouths?

—*Words* by Venus Khoury-Ghata

Point of Origin

There is nothing vast that enters into human life without a curse.

—Sophocles *Antigone*

No true journey can be foreseen. Nor can it be forgotten.

Atticus, not yet born, would remember some words from this journey all his life.

Ben was about to board a train in the early afternoon in Chicago's Union Station. In the Great Hall people were milling about or sitting on benches in the early afternoon light. He looked up. Overhead, he saw the soaring, two hundred feet long, barrel-vaulted skylight rising above the floor. A small black bird flew about.

He noticed two sculpted figures on its East wall, one named 'Day' (holding a rooster) and the other 'Night' (holding an owl), he supposed in recognition of the twenty-four-hour nature of passenger railroading.

Sporting his new tortoiseshell glasses, Ben boarded 'The Empire Builder' in two leaps with only a backpack; space in their sleeping berths would be tight. Nora had winnowed her books down to two. Tommy had forgotten deodorant of all things but Ben said he would share.

Tucked into her clothing, Claire had room for her *Peerless Watercolors*, a pack of playing cards, and a small sketchbook. Sarah brought her laptop but she did not open it, not once.

Ben noticed within minutes that the train journey had begun, not because he felt it but because the station itself had moved. As two trains passed swiftly, he had the sensation that their train was moving backward. These illusions dissolved as the train gained speed.

He felt its size and weight in the acceleration and the sound of clanking metal wheels. The train went North by the city and alongside Lake Michigan, into the suburbs, by trees and houses.

It was Ben who had proposed this journey with four friends he had seen in May at their fortieth college reunion. He had not expected that his group of old friends, so changed he might not have recognized them on the street, had changed so little in their gestures and voices. That strange fitting-togetherness of their small group worked on him again, even with the hubbub and interruptions from former classmates.

They had not had enough time; he wanted to know them again. He proposed a train journey in mid-June 2019, a leisurely trip from Chicago to Seattle, taking advantage of the long summer evenings. The train would be a way to slow time down and get to know one another again in their early sixties. The journey would take three days and two nights.

Yes, Sarah said first. Yes, Tommy would travel from New York; yes, Nora from Dublin; yes, Claire from Paris. He was surprised that they all agreed.

It would be the first overnight train journey for each of them.

Once they settled their gear in their sleeping berths, they gathered in the upper deck's viewing car, where they found a relatively private corner table. They stole glances at one another: Tommy had become bald. That fine head, piercing blue eyes and long Greek nose fitted neatly onto the young man they had known in college.

Nora still had brown eyebrows and brownish hair, but her body was unmistakably that of a woman in her sixties, soft about the middle. Ben, trim and fit, was graying at the temples. Sarah, in her tall elegance, was curiously more herself with straight silver hair. It was strange to see middle age superimposed over youth.

Claire had been redhead with pale freckles in her youth. She still had red hair. Now cut short, it stood up on her head around her cowlicks. She looked like a punk crone or a wizened teenager.

The five friends glanced out the windows and spoke in half sentences, hesitant, sometimes laughing at their first awkward forays into speaking. They reached for their phones as solace and habit as dinner ended. Sarah got out her earbuds, unraveling them from their white case, impatient with the tangles in her rush to disappear into music.

It was Claire who asked them to put aside the phones and to turn off notifications. She'd always been quiet, at best slow to speak. They did not expect this from her. This older Claire, though slightly younger than the others, seemed confident of her request. As she introduced the word game in that first hour together, she spoke as though the game was already unfolding.

She pushed a stray strand of hair from her forehead and brought out a pack of playing cards in a box. The gesture caught their attention and set the scene for what followed.

"Oh," Ben said.

"Oh, indeed," Tommy echoed.

Nora asked, dismayed, "Are you proposing that we play card games?"

Claire explained that with this deck, or any ordinary deck for that matter, any random card could represent a letter of the alphabet by using the *Mirdek Card Cipher System*. And with that simple statement, she explained what they would call 'The Word Game.'

"Each card," she explained, "corresponds to a letter of the alphabet: black Ace-King corresponds to *A-M*, and red Ace-King to *N-Z*."

She paused as they all looked at her blankly.

"The 5 of Spades and the 5 of Clubs both represent *E*, and the Jack of Hearts and of Diamonds both represent *X*. It's easy; each letter corresponds to a number from 1-26."

They still looked bewildered.

"I thought it would help to have a chart," she finished, handing out the *Mirdek* system printed in red and black fonts.

	A	B	C	D	E	F	G	H	I	J	K	L	M
Black	Ace	2	3	4	5	6	7	8	9	10	Jack	Queen	King
	1	2	3	4	5	6	7	8	9	10	11	12	13
	14	15	16	17	18	19	20	21	22	23	24	25	26
Red	Ace	2	3	4	5	6	7	8	9	10	Jack	Queen	King
	N	O	P	Q	R	S	T	U	V	W	X	Y	Z

"Oh, okay," said Tommy. "But what are we do to?"

"I was thinking of a way to reckon with where we are in our lives, you know, a journey at the mid-point in our lives; Dante, without the Inferno?"

Nora quipped, "We are well past mid-way."

Claire persisted, "You pick a card from the top of the deck, keep it hidden, make up a word associated with the letter and tell us a story about an experience. When you're finished, another person begins, until everyone has spoken."

Sarah and Nora glanced at one another and rolled their eyes. "How do we know what the word is, or the letter?" Sarah asked.

"You don't know; the word chosen by the letter can appear anywhere in the first speaker's narration. You tell your story without knowing," Claire said.

Ben was intrigued. It was ingenious, he thought, a single letter and one word would guide the first speaker. It seemed a harmless word game, something that felt contrived at first, but it would give them a new way to know one another.

"When you finish, put this on the table, or we might think you are in a pause, even a long pause," Claire added, placing an old French 10 centime down. It was a beautiful coin.

"Then someone else picks it up to begin speaking, anyone, in any order," she finished.

Constrained by the letters and the word they surmised, what they said surprised them. Sometimes it felt to them more nearly like an unscripted play than a train journey. The word game grew around great silences during their days together on the train. They weighed what was said and not said against the knife-edge of undoing a life each one had built.

Tommy picked the coin up, turning it over to examine it closely. He took the top card from the deck.

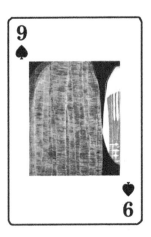

The image surprised Tommy. What was it? Had Claire created an entire deck?

He looked at his *Mirdek* chart and saw that any black nine stood for the letter *I*.

"Imagine this, a family at a dinner table. My father leans over his plate and pounds the bottle of ketchup. My mother hands him a knife to dislodge the flow but he ignores her and pounds vigorously: thump, thump, thump. Frowning, leaning into his task with shoulders stiff, he persists until the front paws and head of a tabby cat emerge. The cat looks a little surprised or maybe indignant to be thumped like a genie from a bottle.

"My father's a scientist, an archaeologist, and he'd just confirmed that my piece of blue shale encases an intact trilobite from the time when the whole plain of the Midwestern United States was an ocean. I picture the Mississippi and Missouri rivers flowing out of their banks into the city, up over curbs and front walks and lawns into Graham Street and the houses here, even this one that's the only one on a hill.

"I see water rising in the kitchen, lapping the edge of the tablecloth. I glance at my sisters, heads bent over their hamburgers, heedless of cats or floods. The cat, entirely dislodged now, shakes itself and turns to lick off the last of the ketchup. I watch its tongue cleave through fur, combing a path back to its tail. A cat-a-comb. I think of making a little joke about this.

"But why bother? No one in my family would get it anyway. 'Would you please pass me the cats-up?' I ask. My dad passed it to me, his face a blank. I suppose this is where

I got my interest in puns, and puns come from the unconscious, you know."

Tommy stopped there. He put the coin on the table.

Sarah stretched out her long legs and said, "I'll go next." She picked up the coin, looked out onto the flat expanse of rural Illinois, and thought for a moment.

"When I think of a table, I see that great tableland of Midwestern America. On a summer's day the sky lifts into the blue-white abyss and comes down on a perfect round edge. You would drop off that edge into sheer black space if you could get there. You are at the center of a turning world. You look from horizon to horizon inside a perfect bowl.

"Spread a checkered cloth of fields over it and pull up a chair and feast your eyes. I must say, I also like a diner's table. It's always Formica. Ideally, you sit in a booth and watch the broad backs of men lined up at the counter, hunched over eggs and bacon. They are eating with purpose because they have somewhere to go, something to do. The waitresses are older than my mother and warmly gruff.

"They slosh coffee into thick mugs and throw down creamers like dice in a game of craps. The first table I had was orange Formica with a pattern of yellow boomerangs. I sat in an orange child's chair and spooned in Cocoa Puffs slowly, one by one, from a blue plastic bowl—while my parents sat apart from me at another bigger table.

"From that lonely world of family, I finally found what I was looking for when I had my own children."

She put the coin back.

Ben cleaned his already immaculate glasses on his shirt tail and spoke next.

"Sometimes I think I only imagined him: my brother. When I was ten and he was eight, he could read two books to my every one. I was knock-kneed and sang off-key. He sang in the boys' choir. He won a prize for the best short story about a dog at school. I ran my bicycle into a light post and ruined my new glasses. He conjugated Latin verbs with gusto.

"I sang the French songs off-key, and never mind the Latin. My hair was messy and my handwriting illegible. Even as a kid, I could already imagine him calling home from Harvard to consult my father about his classes. I saw myself in a ghostly blue light, always failing. And then we traded places. He got killed in a car accident when I was twelve.

"It was as if I knew all along that we would trade places, and then I'd have to erase him. Proust erased his brother, too. I wonder if that's what got me so interested in him as a writer." He looked at his friends, who simply looked back.

He pushed the coin to the middle of the table.

Claire took the coin. Who had been erased for her, she wondered.

"I flatten out the rag-tag dollar bill, insert old George ever so carefully into the metal tray, and feed him into the machine, lifting my fingertips at the last second. My sister is already sorting the laundry into darks, lights, and whites on the wide table. The washers are almost all filled and chugging. It's already eighty-nine degrees outside, so finishing this chore in the morning is a good plan.

"I hand over the coins, keeping one for my Coke, and stand in the doorway. The cold bottle sweats in my hands. Directly in front of me is a small, rounded gas pump, red, like something right out of a Hopper painting. Across Euclid Avenue Mr. Madsen limps by Kean Drug, and on the corner, kids are sharing out lengths of licorice whips they got at Martin's Variety. In front of the Majestic Restaurant the paper man moves about on his corner.

"He nods his head in time with one step forward, the rolled paper extended, thirty-five cents dropped in his palm, and one pace back for the next paper. It's freshly folded before he turns back to the street. In the hot sun, his black brow drips. He wipes his neck with a blue handkerchief. His rounded shoulders repeat the rounded gas pumps.

"Suspenders hold up khaki pants and loop over his gray-white shirt. I want to sketch the slope of his back in motion. He does not speak. To those going by, he's not there, unless they want a paper. And even then, he's not there, only the paper proffered, the waiting hand.

"That was the case for me, too. I could see him to draw him but I knew nothing of the man himself, not even his name. You could say that I erased him, or that I was blind."

She pushed the coin toward Nora.

Nora quipped, "I have no idea what the word was, or is. Oh, alright, I have something." She picked up the coin and turned it over in her hand, fingering its embossment.

"I'm almost always with him because my father's blind. He has a guide dog trained in Athy, a small town about an hour outside of Dublin, and I have a pure black cat from Newtown Mount Kennedy. He got the dog six months ago, just before we emigrated. My father's a musician: he plays the fiddle. I sit at a table by the window in the Majestic Restaurant.

"It's a diner, nothing majestic to it, but the Greeks who run it know my dad by now and he likes to come here for breakfast. People want to call him Donald, and he's forever repeating, 'No, DO, as in donut; it's Donal.' His dog, Fin, is under the table. We call him Fin 'cause we used to walk in Bray by the water, and I'd say, 'There's a big fin out there.'

"My dad would say, 'Step quick, or he'll have you.' He'd reach back his hand for me to grab and we'd run. I was his guide then, running next to the gray sea. But most of the time, he didn't need any guide at all. He knew Dublin in the dark by heart, better than his mates. Sometimes the scraping of chairs hurts Fin's ears and he raises his head, but mostly he's bored. Head on paws, he blinks at the shoes and closes his eyes for a catnap.

"As a child, I thought it odd to call it that when it's a dog sleeping."

Nora finished speaking, looked down at her hands with their wrinkles and no rings, then at Tommy. "Well, what was the word?"

Tommy laughed. "None of you guessed it! It doesn't matter, does it? It's better this way, not knowing, having to listen very carefully to guess. And another thing: no questions, none. No comments about the stories during the game, or at any time. No chit-chat about it, okay?"

They nodded, without knowing why, without realizing how far speaking this way could go. At this moment, they didn't imagine the future. The game and the motion of the train gave them the illusion of only an unfolding present.

When the train stopped in Wisconsin Dells in the late afternoon for refueling, they got off and went to the Stone-

Cold Creamery. They ordered waffle cones of homemade ice-cream. It was odd to be on *terra firma* and Ben missed the rocking of the train, that distinctive clicking of the cars that becomes like the sound of a clock in a house—you don't hear it after a while, but if it's silent, you hear the silence.

Walking the streets in bright sunshine, Sarah saw Trump signs and said how much she admired the president.

Nora's eyebrows shot up, "You must be joking!" Ben made a face and turned away.

Tommy stepped in: "One more rule: no politics in the word game or around it. We can't start judging one another! It would stop the game." They agreed, no politics.

They found a picnic table to play the game (of course they'd brought the coin and cards). Nora licked her mint ice-cream flat into its cone, holding the coin. Counting out the letters from the red portion of the Mirdek chart, she arrived at the letter *P*.

"So much possibility! I went to Ted Drewes with my friend, Kathy, and her dad that first summer in St. Louis. I remember looking at the long lines up to the serving windows that snaked out onto Chippewa Avenue. For the first time I am part of some larger possibility, part of America, I guess. Hopping from foot to foot in my new *Keds* and shorts, you can't tell me apart from the hordes of kids with parents under a dark sky in the heat of a summer night.

"We are all waiting for our concretes from the menu of possibilities. Oh, what were they? Hawaiian, Dutchman, Oreo, Chocolate Chip...I'd never seen such choices in Ireland. But they didn't have brown bread ice-cream. You can turn the cup upside down and it won't fall out Kathy tells me, but I don't want to try it. I don't want to speak, even to say what I want, because everyone will hear my 'accent' and know I am a foreigner, an impostor.

"I want to pretend for a little longer that this is my father, not the man at home with his dog. It is a curious thing to discover in this moment that in my father's absence, I feel I am being watched. It's as if his blindness gives him a kind of uncanny surveillance of me. And though he's not here, I feel he knows what I'm thinking and doing.

"I am immediately unnerved, and suddenly, I'm up to the window. I whisper my choice: a small chocolate-chip concrete."

Biting into her now dripping cone, Nora put the coin down on their table.

Sarah took it and remembered going to Ted Drewes with her children.

"When the kids are six and three, we load them up in our little Volkswagen Bug, and head out to Ted Drewes. It is the only place they want to go for ice-cream in St. Louis, and Jenny wants her stuffed dog to come along. That little dog goes with her almost everywhere. We give them kiddie cones and Jenny insists on 'feeding' the dog. You can well imagine the mess of that!

"Remember those little cups of free water? I fill several of them and bring them back to mop up the dog, and it helps—a little.

"Later, I take him away from her after she's asleep and throw him into the washer and dryer. There are days of crying. He doesn't look right, or smell right, and she wants her old dog back. She's six years old, and I can't imagine how she doesn't seem to get it that the washed dog is the same old dog.

"You try to see what you did that may have opened a fissure, then a crack, then a chasm, and what you might have done differently. As a mother, you think and rethink things like this."

She put the coin down. Tommy took it up, noticing it had become sticky.

Tommy wondered if the word had been Ted or Drewes; nothing else came to mind. He considered 'D'—dog? Probably not.

"Sometime in my third year of analysis, I was having dreams about Ted Drewes. I associated to hot fudge, banana boats, but the dream never opened anything of use to me. I was always a little kid in this dream, out with my family. This was New York, so my analyst didn't get Ted Drewes.

I try to explain, 'It's like vanilla ice-cream, only smoother, flavored with honey.'

"He doesn't respond. I have another dream, and in this dream, my mother is killing my father. His throat is bleeding where she's cut him and he can't do anything but whisper his curses. My mother looks over at me and as I swallow a scoop of ice-cream, it is as if she is appealing to me for something, but I don't know what. I waken with a headache, an ice-cream headache, we used to call it.

"My analyst says, 'Cut her. I scream.' He pauses between those two phrases. I laugh at his weird pause between words, but I stop myself because it's so strange, your tears streaming back along your temples."

He cleaned the coin with water on his napkin and put it down.

Claire followed the others to Ted Drewes in a very roundabout way.

"I never went there as a little kid; I didn't go to Ted Drewes until I was a teenager. But I have another ice-cream experience. I went to a party with my sister, but my mother was also there, so it must have been a family thing, not a children's party.

"I am spinning around in circles in my underpants, just filled with excitement, unable to hold still. My mother corners me and says, 'Arms up.' A cool swish of cotton slip falls over my head, muffling the light. Then the dress, pale pink, and my arms are allowed down. I finger the white smocking and turn to my sister, Mary.

"We button each other up the back, and then there's the sash, my mother's job. She struggles with it, trying bow after bow until it hangs limp like a rumpled tail. I sit on the floor and pull on my new anklet socks and buckle my Mary-Janes with five-year-old expertise.

"At the party, there are children, screaming, racing, raucous, snotty, pushing, they run in packs. I want to be alone under blue summer sky. I stand on the porch with a bowl of chocolate ice-cream and someone races by, bumping my elbow. The chocolate runs all over the front of my dress. I go inside, blinded in the sudden dark, and reach up to put my bowl in the sink. It is quiet in here.

"I walk around the house. I follow the stairs up to a big bathroom of green and white tiles, cool as a basement. It is flooded with light.

"It never crosses my mind to wash my dress. I pull the sash apart and throw it to the floor. I unbuckle my shoes and put them on the bathmat, followed by socks. Ooh, lovely cool tiles on bare feet. Now the buttons—no problem with the top two and the bottom two, but I can't reach the one in the middle of my back. I tug the dress up and seek that button. I yank.

"Finally, I pull my arms inside and wiggle out, shimmy the dress over my head and fling it off. I wander around over the bathmat, up on the side of the tub. I climb on the toilet and up onto the sink. I pull myself up and stand. There in the mirror, I see a girl without a head. I open the mirror and there are rows of things to play with.

"Carefully, squatting and then standing, I line them up on the back of the sink: pill bottles, creams, lipsticks, tweezers, q-tips. They are possibilities for an art project on a new scale. A knock—oh no, not now; 'I'm using it,' I shout, and steps retreat. I climb down. I line up pills on the tiles, yellows alternating with blues. I bring out the lipstick, mark my arms and legs in bold, oily stripes.

"I take the lid off the cream and push my finger into the jar. There's another knock and my mother's voice, calling out my name."

Claire put the coin down and glanced at Ben.

Ben picked up the coin but did not speak. He thought to himself: whatever it is you yearned for only held a place for something else you imagined, a souvenir of something lost that you couldn't explain or get back, even as a child, something you'll likely go on searching for all your life.

He wanted to tell them how Proust captures the absurdity of wanting a particular thing or experience so vividly that he moves away from realizing his desires. He does this because when he finally gets to have an experience he's waited for, it's almost inevitably disappointing. He learns this, even as a young child.

But at this point, Ben was still afraid to talk about Proust, afraid they would dismiss him and what was the most important thing in his life—not an event, or a person, but a work of fiction in three thousand pages. This conjecture, with its accusation, was outside the word game.

"I have nothing to add, and we're running late," he said, looking at his watch, handing the coin and cards to Claire.

They had forgotten the time entirely and had to race back to the train in a single taxi, with a driver who thought it wonderful to perch Claire on Tommy's lap in the front and cram the rest of them in the back. Tommy could smell the freshness of her shampoo, very like his wife's scent. Then they were stalled for an hour on the tracks for something to be loaded on the train.

Sarah dallied by an open window, tense in her shoulders, irritable. Nora watched the clouds gather, piling up in high gray and gray-white stacks, back lit with an on-coming storm. The sky rendered the train and town and railway station small. By the time they pulled out, rain slashed the windows.

It rained all through dinner, luxurious with wine, flowers, white tablecloth, and cloth napkins. They crossed over the Mississippi River and spent most of that hour laughing at the slightest thing. If they had been children, they'd have raced through the train or picked a fight.

When the train made a stop in Minneapolis at 8pm to take on new passengers, Sarah suggested they return to the word game on the upper deck. She did not expect to like the game at all, and yet here she was, impatient to return, to go further.

Sarah took the coin as she sat, following the red cards in the second half of the alphabet, to *O*.

"Okay. When I'm having sex, I try to stop that awful chatter that goes on in my head all the time. Especially lists. I remember once making a list of groceries, and when I got to the Cheerios, I started to laugh. I laughed until I got the hiccups. Jack couldn't figure out what had come over me.

"I think of his bare knees sometimes. I see leggy bursts of yellow and orange, nasturtiums rocking in the wind—and his knees. I think of a time when we were out driving in his old van. We'd stopped at a lake. I reached over and touched him behind his right knee and we made love right then. I've never really let go like that again.

"Someone came and looked in the window at us. A couple of boys, I think. I can't remember this part very clearly. Jack got out to chase them away and when he came back, I couldn't bear the idea of beginning again. It's odd that I almost always see his knees—as if they were a last outpost."

She paused and put the coin down.

Ben thought Sarah's word was obvious. He smiled and tilted his head in thought.

"I see things in the dark: the outline of our clothing in a lump on the chair, a south-facing window and its deep sill, the ceiling beams, as if they are holding up the house for us. An old, paneled door we had dipped to take off the layers of paint. I see its hinges and markings on the wood that I know by heart. It is hard to breathe deeply. I gasp in the shallows.

"I wonder if I'll crush him; no, I think I've crushed him already. I don't want to see his face, to see the devastation in his eyes that appears out of nowhere. I turn and there's the lamp, the shade and pedestal in gray, even though they're not. I am relieved when it's over, more than just spent, relieved that it didn't devastate him. I think about my brother and why I am the one to live.

"Why can't I make love without thinking of this question? Sometimes it's just too much for me and I turn away from Carl abruptly, or get up and go to another room."

Ben sighed. "That's all." He slid the coin to the center of the table and overshot, so that it landed in Nora's lap. They laughed.

Nora thought the word was sex or love but rejected that trajectory. She went another way.

"I can't claim sex was ever a very intense interest. No, I mean that. But I've felt things very early in my life that have become engrained in my body and marked me.

"When I was five, I had a terrible flu. My mother made a poultice and rubbed it on my chest and back. She tore up old sheets and wrapped me. She sat me up and rocked me forward a little each time the material rounded my back. She whispered, 'There, love,' and was very gentle; yet I expected her to make me well and she couldn't.

"I heard my father tuning his fiddle and called out for him, but my mother came instead. And I wanted him. Then it was always him, not her, who came to me.

"She died of that flu. My father was like a statue for weeks. He stopped playing. My body holds a longing for the sound of his fiddle, the strange changes of key in his tuning, almost a crying out. My mother was wearing a blue dress when she nursed me. I can see its folds, the inside of the elbow where the cloth creases. It was a dress with blue flowers, dark blue.

"I see lights swirling, and medicine bottles, hear the clink of cutlery from the kitchen, see the open fire and my father mute as a statue. We got Fin and moved to St. Louis after that.

"But I didn't get over what happened. Over here I heard a couple of girls singing a jump rope jingle: 'I had a little bird, her name was Enza. I opened the window. And in flew Enza.' I started to scream at them, just went wild, as if their song could make it all happen again.

"Oh, there were men I loved. But I loved them from a distance. I've been afraid that sex is an exchange in which you get something you didn't bargain for, you know, that sex really does link up with death. That's it, as far as I can go right now."

She put the coin down.

Claire noticed that they were now passing through a city, a cityscape of lit buildings. St. Paul? The rain had cleared and sky was deepening toward indigo, toward night. She began:

"I didn't have sex until I was in my thirties. It was so new and amazing to me. But, you know, when you get to that moment of orgasm, let's face it, you are as far from each other as it's possible to get. Nora, your description of your mother makes me think of that game we played as children. You marched around and went under an arch of arms, and then the arms came down on you and rocked you back and forth: *London bridges falling down.*

"You must cooperate but you are not in charge of your body. Sex is so much like that! Light filters through the

31

layers of copper beech in our backyard. John's face and body are like a new country. I cross over, not as a tourist, nor as a native, but as someone traveling into the unknown."

She put the coin back.

Tommy looked down at his fingers, surprised that he needed a nail clipper.

"Sometimes it's hard to work out the time. Julie's ready to go late at night, just when I'm drifting into sleep. At 6am, when I'm alert and frisky, she's sound asleep and grumpy if awakened. We finally settled on the time before dinner, but her day's end and mine do not always coincide. Then there's dinner to cook, which I like to do as a way of coming down from my day, chopping things, and listening to music.

"She likes to go to aerobics before dinner. Between her schedule and mine, it's hard to catch up with one another. So, we have sex rarely, maybe only once a month or so. When we get to it though, it's terrific. She touches one little place on me, almost any place, and my whole body responds. I imagine lions playing, their golden coats and rippling muscles. Oh yeah, we roar!"

He put the coin down next to the cards.

They said goodnight suddenly, each heading to their own sleeping quarters, as though they'd said too much, or perhaps too little of too much.

Sarah, Nora, and Claire had a large bedroom with two stacked beds and a fold-out single bed. Tommy and Ben slept in bunks a car away.

There is nothing like falling asleep on a train. From her berth, Claire saw houses in the distance as tiny glimmers of light floating by in vast space. She'd listened to stations called out during the day, but the announcements had stopped, and she'd lost these coordinates of space. Where were they? Leaving Central Time? She imagined mountains ringing a valley.

Fields and streams and houses slept under a dome of stars out there. The train moved along, as if a sentient being, searching the distances, never arriving, always in pursuit of another place and experience.

Sarah was sleepy but did not fall into sleep quickly. Catch phrases like tufts of cotton wool, pulled at coherent thought. Voices came to her: *wouldn't you know…oh, he does…she was just standing there…oh yeah, (a sharp intake of breath), terrible…that's not the point. Words become unmoored from their anchors: cats, ketchup, nasturtiums, in flew Enza.*

Nora turned on her side and thought of knees as a last outpost.

In his upper berth, Tommy was thoughtful. He thought about the weighty, real traces of words on the body, how words trigger something else: an excitation or shutting down, that can last for decades. The body becomes sexual in exchange for a word, a voice, or a glance.

When you really consider it, sex is just a path in which you get a glimpse into what has already happened a long time ago, when one bodily moment became a code for something else, something that's otherwise so submerged in us we hardly know it's there at all.

Ben was restless, his body just a bit too long. He had to curl up to sleep, sticking his feet out. He drifted in and out of sleep, snoring lightly beneath Tommy.

Sarah wakened just as 'Good Morning, we are entering Minot, North Dakota,' was announced. She must have overslept; no, they'd just gained an hour going away from Central Time overnight. She nonetheless jostled Nora and Claire awake and headed into the shower.

The five gathered for breakfast in the dining car, a feast of French toast, bacon, eggs, and fresh, hot coffee. This time, it was Tommy who wanted to get to the game. "Hey, Claire, did you bring the cards?" She raised her eyebrows and took a slow bite of her egg; no, she had not.

The train passed by open, flat Northern prairies, empty expanses under a blazing sun and a wide sky. They went by ghost towns.

When they gathered upstairs, Tommy picked up the coin and a card from the stack. His cardinal-in-a-snowstorm Queen of Clubs, led him to an *L*, launched them into the next round.

"I look down at my leg, one knee crossed over the other, and this leg, this shoe, seems to belong to someone else—another man sitting in a waiting room by a lamp. On the table beside the lamp, I notice a bowl of flowers. The bowl is matt black and shallow, with a wide mouth, maybe a foot across. I measure the lie of a lake from shore to shore. I was here because my training as an analyst demanded that I begin with my own analysis.

"The door opens and a tall man speaks in a soft voice, 'Mr. Somers?' I smile a little at this name as if it's not my name. He speaks and vanishes, leaving the door open, and I follow. He is already sitting in a chair at the head of a couch with a rug at its foot. I can nearly see the imprint of the last body, and I want to laugh at that—the last body—and the idea of me lying down here seems like a form of dying.

"I choose the single chair across the room from his. I study the rug where it meets the polished golden boards of the room and the edge of his cherry bookcases. His books declare him a reader of Freud in German, Lacan in French, and Harrari in Spanish.

"I wonder what in the world to say. 'I suppose it's up to me to begin,' I say. He says nothing, no refutation, nor confirmation. 'Well, if you're not going to reply, why am I here?' I ask. He doesn't answer that and there's a small fluttering inside my stomach, a wave against the edge of a sloop that tips into vertigo before the boat rights itself.

"For a moment, it is like hearing myself speaking in a room alone, my voice going out into the air without answer, and in that moment, I am already in a panic.

"Can I carve out of these silences the analyst I want him to be? Who is that? Someone who might tolerate me at first, then maybe love me—love me for what, I would show him, were all the wrong reasons. I would try to settle into his silence; I would do anything just to hear his voice. 'What do you want from me?' I ask. No answer. 'I don't know what to do here. Should I lie down on the couch?'

"'Should I lie?' he says back. 'Yeah. This first time, should I lie down on the couch?' He shrugs and I take that as permission. I sit down on the couch and think about taking off my shoes, but don't. I lay back with my shoes tilted out into a *V* shape on the little foot rug. I can hear the clock ticking. This does not make things better. I start to go over things I could say and discard every idea. 'That's all for today,' he says.

"I remember I stood so fast the floor tilted. Crossing to the door, I wanted to get out. I stomped down the walk and out the gate and everything on a June morning in New York passed in a blur of sun, brick sidewalks, people storming past, a child dripping her popsicle. What had happened? I'd said virtually nothing, nothing of any importance anyway.

"I walked into a coffee shop took a stool by the window with my coffee, trying to understand why I was so angry. He'd done nothing, said nothing. Actually, he'd said, 'Should I lie?' And that really was the first question of my analysis. I'd been thinking of it as a training analysis and I hadn't intended to be truthful about anything.

"I was trying to consider the safest hiding place and— my intention to lie was perfectly evident to him. I thought he was brilliant."

He smiled to himself and put the coin back.

Ben was puzzled. He took up the coin. Was Tommy's word look or lie?

"'Look, it's snowing,' my mother says. I look up; a fine powder flies slanting against the bark of the tree outside our kitchen window. First, there's a staccato of snow on dark bark, then just bits of bark show through, and then, the whole trunk is embedded. I can barely see the trees at the end of the yard, just the outlines, sweeping in and out, depending on the wind.

"That winter, after his funeral, it snowed and the snow filled up the streets, filled up my brother's footprints. My parents emptied his room, painted it, and brought in my things; and there I was, as if he'd never been there. Secretly, I hated my brother, my brilliant brother whom I also loved. After his death, I tried to forget him, pretending that I was an only child.

"I'm not telling you why, and that's another lie, a lie of omission, which you'd think is just a little, minor lie, the kind of thing we do all day long every day to save ourselves. But in this case, the omission is the main truth of it."

He removed his glasses and put the coin down.

Sarah said, "This is a strange game, Claire." She thought for a moment.

"I was five when I learned there's no Santa Claus. I was just devastated by that, so I was determined my children would believe for as long as possible. When James, my youngest, was six, he went through all the questions: 'How does Santa get around the whole world in one night? Lots of houses have no chimney, so how does he get in? That Santa in Famous Barr is a fake; maybe every Santa is a fake, Mom.'

"And I had my replies ready: 'Supersonic Sleigh, Model GMX4, very, very fast; he has a magical pass key to every home in the world; and yes, all those Santas are fakes, because of course, the real one's at the North Pole, busiest season, you know, and elf productivity down ten percent this year—it was on the news, didn't you hear it?' I think he believed me, despite his misgivings.

"A year later, I'd had a hysterectomy. Uterine cancer, very contained, no radiation, just a lot of follow-up visits. I'd told the children there was nothing to worry about but James didn't believe me. He worried so much, he was throwing up every morning. At seven! When he started in with the questions that year, I just couldn't let him lose Santa. 'Mom, really, isn't Santa just you and Dad?'

"'With all my hospital bills, you think we can afford to be Santa Claus?' I joked. It was a terrible lie for so many reasons, mostly because it was true that we didn't have much money. His grandparents were chipping in for Christmas, a loan that Jack insisted we'd pay back. But James bought it—he believed. Sometimes lying is necessary. But there's a cost too; you lose someone's trust, even if he believes you."

She put the coin down.

"How did you know he believed you?" Nora began, only to see Tommy shake his head.

Nora held the coin and thought.

"When I remember Dublin, I wonder if I can believe my memories. I see bridges over somber water and bicycles everywhere, not as recreation, as the main way of getting around the city. I used to go on the crossbar with Danny, my cousin, into Stephen's Green in the summer. I remember Halloween and going around the streets of Stoneybatter, where we lived, in a witch costume, collecting apples and sweets.

"But no one does Halloween like that in Ireland, certainly not in the 1970s! We'd have music and singing, and brack with things hidden inside the cake, a ring, a shilling, something else. See, I can't remember it—it's like something you've made up to fit a life you think you once lived that doesn't belong to you. I must have worn the witch costume here, after we moved.

"People think math is all about facts, things that are both true and indisputable, but that's not so. Once you get into negative numbers, you've left the realm of correspondences between what you see and can map out and measure—it's about infinity really. The great mathematicians are always pushing off further in that direction.

"At first negative numbers were abhorrent to most mathematicians. Maybe they sensed they were going to find out just how much we create a universe out of nothing: God, religion, and all. Anyway, it's made me worry a lot less about what's real or not in my memories. Maybe it's not a matter of truth or lies. It's just that there are aberrations."

She put the coin back.

Claire looked out the train window at cows, tiny as ants, roaming a wide field somewhere in Idaho. She looked back to her waiting friends and picked up the coin.

"As a child, I was part of a whole atmosphere of aberrations in light and color. Sometimes I still experience a heightened vision and then a landscape can become almost eerily alive, replacing what was there. I remember when this happened the first time. A certain light, beautiful and glaring, covered the playground—and I could recognize nothing as familiar, nor could I name a single person. It was a theft of time, a theft of myself.

"It was as if the light itself took me over, took me in its grasp, and removed me from the scene. And now, I have the feeling that light looks through me when I paint. I am painting a landscape, let's say, and I am the landscape the light is painting. Aberrations are me at my most truthful."

Tommy went alone to the rear viewing car. All the seats faced out. Trees flashed by, shifting on a light wind. What was it like to be Claire? What did she see when she looked at the world? He had so many questions but the game had no questions. Tommy remembered how she'd disappeared for months at a time in college.

He knew so little, in fact, about these friends. He wondered if it was the word game that made it possible for Ben to talk about his brother for the first time in his life, and the fact that they didn't ask, they didn't comment, not then, and not ever while on the train.

At noon they crossed into Montana and gathered in the dining car for lunch. Nora sipped from her glass of water, squinting in the bright light that fell through the window, spliced by the tall trees they passed. They selected salads and sandwiches. Sarah noticed a family with two teenagers, or she surmised they were a family. The boy and girl ate at a table across from the parents.

All four were on their phones. Sarah was grateful of the agreement on the first day not to check devices beyond once a day. But it was harder than she supposed to unhook herself from playing games on her phone, from scrolling, reading the latest news, reading messages, sending WhatsApp texts, and checking emails.

After lunch they moved to a cleared table on the upper deck. Claire brought out the deck of cards and the coin. Immediately, Ben took the card on top and turned it over.

He checked the *Mirdek*, cleared his throat, and began.

"My family made a clutter in my mind. Their voices telegraph through mine. Benjamin, where is your baseball? Follow the stitches flying into the glove, not onto the ground. Show us you can be the star-player. Instead, you pick up a trombone. And that sound cuts your father the loudest, as if your hook found the wrong fish. And always say yes like you mean it, even when your whole boy body protests. Here is a sink-full of boats. Look at them with your calculator eyes.

"Can you swim out to the boats? You have a small bony skeleton, Benjamin; everything about you is small. You try to smash your smallness into a trophy, into something to say that you are exactly like your brother. But you are your mother's boy, a hen's Ben, your body an elevator lifting to meet her eyes stuck between the floors. Your body is a telegraph, signaling hers, and there's no hiding from that."

He stopped, still holding the coin, and then put it down.

Tommy wondered if Ben was imitating the voices of family members or talking about himself to himself.

Nora was excited to speak about clutter.

"When I think of clutter, I think of elegance. I think of patterns in what may look like something random—small multiples that lay out a scope of variations—and the exponential complexity of negative shapes. I can see a line of clothes pegs like pictographs in ghostly variations. I think of Josef Albers' and his demonstration that 1+1 is equal to 3 or more.

"All sorts of combinations can show up by changing the positions of what you see in negative space. Think of two parallel bars: the space between and around them opens into three. Cross the bars and there are four quadrants, four spaces.

"And it isn't only visual, or even mostly visual for me. I hear my father's fiddle, a kind of ear training that began before I was born. I hear the way he practices arpeggios, keeping time in a pattern with variations. His fingers move with the sound, his foot taps. I love that elegance in the world: a grid over what I see and hear, a harmony in which I come to exist.

"I don't know what I mean by that! It's not the idea of clutter as mess that draws me, but of clutter as new combinations, and me belonging to them, in a family of things: $1 + 1 = 3$ or more."

Nora put the coin down.

Sarah lifted her hair, spun it into a knot, and pinned it. Then she picked up the coin.

"I do think of a mess. I think of the kitchen counter on school mornings. Composition books slide over a Mickey-Mouse watch missing its strap, and there's a line of marshmallows, peanut butter, and mounds of pickle relish in paper cups next to the Wonder Bread bag, opened with soft bread poking out, ready to be assembled into sandwiches, but the lunchboxes are still in the sink.

"Jenny's chart of home heating fuels in the US in 1990 has fallen to the floor, where someone has left a flashlight serving as a paperweight on a pile of papers. Her bacon from breakfast congeals on a note 'save it for my afternoon snack.' James has left his box of color-aid on the stool next to his shin guards.

"Nowhere in that picture is any idea that I might exist, that I might be a person. And I cling to my complaints about the clutter every day because it affirms that I am their mother; at least I am that. Clutter comes from the idea of clotting, as in blood coagulating. As in 'Blood runs thicker than water.'"

She put the coin down near Tommy.

Tommy hesitated, ran his left hand over his mouth, and began.

"When I think of clutter, I think of distraction; all my life this has been my nemesis. On this day, there was too much clutter in my shoulder bag. I stood at the check-in counter under the mint-white lights, stirring a little sugar into my cup of coffee, but where to discard the wooden stirring stick? I was searching through my bag, my wallet, my coat, my pants' pockets for our passports, or maybe it was our tickets.

"The line pressed in behind us, and I could feel the impersonal impatience of the hoard, which only made me fumble more. My wife was going to meet us and I'd put my daughter in her stroller after she'd played on the floor and climbed all over our suitcases. When I went to fold up her stroller, I missed her. I looked up to see a woman carrying her, a woman with long red hair, moving along at a clip, not my wife.

"I couldn't make sense of this image and stood there, a doctor of do-little-or-nothing in the face of a crisis. My legs were sandbagged, and then a cry rang out from my throat, but it was too late to stop what had already happened. She was two. I remember her walking ahead of me in her red coat, white tights, little black shoes. I see the gait of her steps as a dance again and again as she moves from the front door of our brownstone to the taxi.

"I did not see her again. All because of my distractibility, my tendency to get lost in clutter, to create it as if to take refuge from something worse. Then the worst happened. Oh God, I'll stop now."

And with that, Tommy got up and left the car, taking the coin with him.

Sarah said, "Look, I know, no questions, no comments, but shouldn't I go see if he's alright?"

Nora replied, "But we know he isn't alright. Let's let him be."

They sat in silence then, waiting for him to come back. Sarah was caught in her anguish for him and yet she agreed that it would betray him to go after him, or to speak in his absence. And he did return after long thirty minutes, bearing a tray of teacups and cookies, coming with a slanting, slow walk and shy grin, his eyes a wreck of red.

He cleared his throat. "Please continue," he said, putting the coin down.

But they took a long break and did not resume the game until much later. Nora and Sarah went to the viewing car with seats that faced outward. Tommy and Ben went to their berth and sat across from one another.

Claire wandered through the train and chose a table on the upper deck to sketch passengers.

The train was passing through Northern Montana. It had all afternoon. Each, from their own vantage point, looked out onto the Rocky Mountains, the Columbia River. The train went around curves; it went in and out of East Glacier Park, and West Glacier Park.

They passed woods in full leaf, air suffused with light cut suddenly off by a mountain pass or a tunnel, colors they could not pin down, thousands of individual sounds within the train itself, voices all around them from fellow travelers. And these things allowed them to absorb what Tommy had spoken.

They ate dinner as a group and stayed together in companionable silence, passing remarks about the train, the scenery, the end of the route coming the next morning.

They were in Whitefish, Montana at sunset before they remembered that Claire had not taken her turn in the last round of the word game. She had had all afternoon and evening to consider what word and what to say. Invited to speak, she hesitated, tilted her head, and began.

"For me, language was the clutter I wanted to simplify and remake. It has little to do with my family. Even though I lived with my mother and sister at the time of my first psychotic crisis, I hardly noticed them. Even before that, before I began hearing voices, I was distracted by the sound-sense of words, and this persisted, insisted over the words I might have chosen voluntarily.

"Words dropped into me out of the blue. They did not come as full sentences, and sometimes I could not finish my sentence. I could only try to speak around these imposed phrases, which frightened me and fascinated me. A pen disappeared as 'pen' and became a 'paperskate,' the mirror became a 'reflector,' my shoes 'foot armor.' And when this happened, the most ordinary things swelled with meaning, cluttering my mind, clustering in new ways by themselves.

"This clutter derailed my thoughts. Sometimes I wondered—what was this language in which things became more alive, more immediate, more perceptibly essences of themselves? I made mistakes with words and invented. I would gather phrases as if they made sense: 'The trees are playing Brahms, my braces are radio conductors, too many ducks to count in the countdown to dying, viaduct.'

"It was a way of speaking, yet *I* wasn't speaking. And then, sometime in my early thirties, I began to hear my word mistakes. I remember I was going to bake a sour cream fudge cake. I asked my sister to buy 'eight inches of pucker cream.' She drew a container on the grocery list. She asked me did I mean 'ounces,' did I mean 'sour' cream. And I heard her, above the other clutter of clusters in my mind, I heard her voice and her words."

Ben was surprised at Claire's strange experience with language. However, they all heard things oddly. He'd begun with the letter *T* and chosen 'telegraph' as his word—yet everyone thought the word was 'clutter.' He wondered at that—how the mind hears a word and settles on that word and stops listening. Had this been happening all along?

In fact, the game did not specify that they would be *required* to guess the letter and the original word after the first speaker, but that was what they all did. And they listened and spoke this way from the start, as though this puzzled, close listening was integral to the game itself. And then it was.

Tommy realized that the word game was having effects. They had needed a spell of decompression after his exit, and now again after Claire's contribution. Each one was in their sleeping quarters by 10pm. Lying in his berth the last night on the train, he remembered that European bunks on a night train are usually set at ninety degrees to the direction of travel like lines on a ruler, creating a side-to-side rocking movement.

Here the bunks were arranged in the direction of travel, so that falling asleep, he had the sense of being propelled forward in space. What were they being propelled toward? He could not conjecture what would happen before their arrival in Seattle the next day.

At Spokane, in the middle of the night, the cars of the train going to Seattle were separated from those going to Portland; the train was disassembled and reassembled into two trains. Claire woke up to the racket and wondered if she was on the right train now.

Sarah looked at her watch in the dim morning light: 6:40am. They'd lost another hour. It would be their last morning. She woke them all. The five friends gathered for breakfast at 7:05am, just as the announcement came that they were entering Everett, Washington.

Tommy sipped his coffee and looked out on the misty little town. "I can't believe I slept through crossing the Cascades."

They knew it was impossible to see anything of that stunning mountain range in pitch darkness from the train, whether one was sleeping or awake. Each smiled at Tommy's impossible longing.

They may have each experienced a sense of having gone far enough, for they did not resume the game on the morning of the last day. They packed up their belongings, checked their phones, read, and listened to the stations being called out.

Tommy saw that they had stopped in a small town behind a peak-roofed small railroad station.

Edmund, Washington.

Sarah looked to one side and saw houses and looping telephone wires that seemed to connect them. She looked to the other side into a parking lot, wet cars glinting in sunlight.

Nora traced a cutout pattern of trees against a dark horizon. She noticed things close to the slowing train, gray-white paint peeled from the siding of a building, and window-glass, back lit from a source inside, chalky with dirt.

Claire looked out another window and saw the Puget Sound to her right, and beyond that the trees of Bainbridge

Island, felted blue, and farther out the jagged edge of the Olympia Mountains traced in lilac.

Seattle, Washington.

An immense longing, almost an animal presence, took up residence in Ben. It inhabited him in a town he'd never visited before and came from a place he could not name.

During the Pandemic

During the pandemic, I went outside as into an abstraction,
everybody a vector, every public space a possible inflection
point, the very air a moral injury ...

—Rick Barot

Fool's Gold

Offer unto me that which is very dear to thee—which thou holdest most covetable.

—Bhagavad Gita

Sarah's two grown children had returned, living in their old rooms at Lenox Place. Almost two months had passed since the lockdown began in St. Louis in mid-March 2020; the train journey seemed years ago.

Sarah tucked her new edition of *Crime and Punishment* under her arm and peered into the refrigerator. Had someone eaten the half sandwich she'd saved for lunch? She looked through the French doors to the front walk and marveled at the greenness of the lawns all down Lenox Place, even after a dry spring. Going around to the side of the house, she sat in the glider with her book in the cool of the small maple they'd planted last year.

Suddenly, there was a man, an ordinary man in khaki pants and a gray t-shirt, lifting the garbage lid on the curb can gently, silently. He picked up something from the top and walked away, opening it up and taking a first big bite. That was her half sandwich, she realized.

Back in the kitchen, Sarah's attention turned from her phyllo dough to her daughter. The strudel was a delicate affair, lined up on the counter in neat stacks of twenty-four dry, white rectangular sheets, awaiting intricacy as though she were folding origami papers. She felt herself falter, intent on the stacks, then her daughter.

Jenny sat on her stool glancing over at her mother and then back to a list of private high schools. Sarah looked at the diagrams in her cookbook. Upstairs somewhere fourteen-year-old Tyler, Jenny's daughter, was playing music with the windows open. Sarah could hear the thump of it.

"Mom," Jenny began. "This high school wants the child to apply by 30 May for the fall, at the latest, and then there are two interviews."

"Hmmm, is that so?" 'Phyllo dough dries out quickly once unwrapped,' the cookbook admonished.

"Tyler can read and do math at a 10th grade level already. This one says it caters to children with precocious intellectual passions and gifts. But do you think that Tyler would feel, well, overlooked in such a school?"

'Have melted butter ready,' the cookbook told Sarah, 'before stacking.' She saw that the sheets were already stacked and sticking to one another. She rushed to put a stick of butter into a small saucepan. She bent down, pushing a strand of her hair from her face, to watch the flame flare from the gas burner.

"Mother, are you even listening?"

Jenny put her coffee cup in the sink, rinsed it and put it on the counter.

"Schools may not open anytime soon; there's nothing to really consider yet," Sarah said.

"Oh, Mom, you're such a pessimist. Of course, she should apply now. I'm going to work," Jenny huffed, leaving the school list. She worked as a maternity nurse at Barnes' Hospital. "My shift is over at 5pm, so I'll make it for dinner tonight," she added.

Sarah bristled with irritation as she assembled the strudel. Did Jenny really think that she could assure her child's happiness by picking a particular private school, a school that she was so sure would open during a pandemic? Tyler struggled to stay focused on her remote schooling up in her room. Whenever Sarah checked in on the girl, she was listening to music, or drawing, or both at once.

When the strudel was safely in the oven and the house quiet again, Sarah sat on the stool her daughter had vacated. She missed Jenny as a child; yes, she missed the era in her life when they were both children—when the house was filled with their homework and games and clothes, when they banged the screen door coming and going, their voices shouting out, 'I'm home, Mom' and 'I'm off now, Mom.'

How strange that they were grown, and stranger still to be tired of her family now that they were home again—and she was tired of them. She loved Jenny and James. But they really didn't need her. Jenny would consult with Eric about this high school choice. He was stuck in Italy on a business trip, indefinitely it now seemed. They would make the decision, as it should be. And James would turn twenty-seven this year, she reminded herself.

No one tells us how it happens, she thought, how you are a mother at one moment, an embarrassment at another, and finally quite useless to your children, how they forget how much they once demanded, yes, even as they return home and continue to make demands you can't possibly satisfy.

The cookbook said, 'When painting the butter lightly on each sheet if a few of them pucker or break, it doesn't matter in the overall design. No one's likely to notice them in the layers.' She smiled at this hint of forgiveness.

Sarah rose and climbed the curving, wooden staircase to the second floor. She had been born into this house; it was a second skin to her. She sometimes wondered what it might be like to move. She could not imagine herself doing so. Tommy was in New York City, Ben in Amherst, Nora was back in Dublin, at least for now, and Claire was living in a tiny village in the south of France—what was it called, something starting with a Q?

No, St. Louis was her home, and she was used to wandering daily that navigable, known world. But there was little hope of navigating anywhere now; her friends were going to stay wherever they happened to be in March 2020. For how long, she could not imagine. The world had stopped; in some inconceivable way, it had stopped everywhere.

From the second-floor window, Sarah spotted James sitting in the hammock he'd hung just yesterday. God, he was handsome in his shorts and t-shirt. She considered the unknown man searching in garbage for food, hesitated, then went into her son's room and opened his closet, her eyes adjusting to the dark. She wondered if he'd miss an unused Christmas sweater. Was it hers to give? James may not even notice.

Sarah loved the attic: three generations of memories resided under its wide eaves. As a child, she'd played up here in the maze of trunks, boxes, old mirrors, and a tall, broken grandfather clock. The air was hot and Sarah broke into a light sweat. After two hours of sorting and assembling her bundles, she opened one last trunk. It was Jenny's.

Sarah found not only the clothes of a teenager but also a stuffed giraffe, mittens, and every pair of dungarees the child ever wore, starting at age four. They were Oshkosh mostly. Sarah lifted each pair and refolded and stacked them. She sang, "Out of my window looking through the night, I can see the bar-ges' flickering light." She coughed in the dusty air.

"Silently flows the river to the sea, and the barges, too, go si-lent-ly." Jenny used to cringe when Sarah sang—but she never asked her mother to stop. Sarah put the dungarees into a plastic bag. With parents out of work, there were children in St. Louis who could use them.

Sarah went online to look for places open for clothing donations and found only one, way out in St. Charles, with specified hours for a 'contactless delivery.' Maybe tomorrow, she thought, but for now, she would just order groceries. She found the home delivery option for her favorite grocery store: Straubs at the corner of Kingshighway and Maryland Avenue.

This neighborhood store was small, and she knew every aisle by heart. She used to go sometimes just to look at things and be recognized.

All that was over for now. Although others might stand in a long, snaking line to enter the store in small numbers, Sarah did not risk it. But she remembered, as if from another country, the butcher, Michael, asking, "How can I help you today, Sarah?" Indeed, could *anyone* help now? Well, she could still order steaks for the grill.

She wondered if Michael, unseen, would still trim the fat from the edges. She missed going out to get groceries.

She was fortunate not to worry about the cost, selecting what she wanted for dinner that night from her screen.

She turned to the pastry selections. What an array, all photographed to look inviting: Chocolate Mousse, Cup Crème Brulé, Floating Island, Key Lime Tart, Lemon Meringue, Linzer Tart, Paris Brest Peach Tart, Pecan Bourbon Tart, Black Forest Cake, Chocolate Pear Delice, Golden Triangle, Key West Lemon Fig Delight, Sachertorte, Tiramisu. Each name seemed so seductive and precarious.

There were birthday cakes too, roses blooming in pink and yellow, waiting for the greetings to be inscribed, for sprinkles and candles. She'd bought birthday cakes for each of her children here for years. Was it so terrible to seek some enjoyment, some little comfort in a world filled with a thousand dangers and limits and impossible yearnings? But she had her strudel.

The front doorbell chimed. The Insta-cart man, not a young man, walked away as Sarah opened the door. She'd left his tip in an envelope, despite the expense of the delivery itself. She called out her thanks. He raised a hand in salute without turning back.

Sarah took the groceries out of their bags and placed them on the tile floor just inside the door, taking the bags out to the trash right away. Then she sat on a low stool in the foyer and wiped each package with disinfectant wipes. Mail fell through the letter box onto the floor. She put it out in the fresh air to decontaminate it for forty-eight hours, as suggested by her friend, Maggie. One could not be too careful with this virus.

Sarah poured herself a glass of chilled Sancerre and began a familiar routine. She washed the crystal and dried each glass, seeing her mother's hands in her own hands. She wiped the dining room table and shook a clean linen cloth over it and laid out five napkins and place settings. Then she stood still, irritated by her unease and growing sense of guilt.

But why should she feel guilty? She'd done nothing wrong. She'd done nothing. She made a leafy salad in the big, deep wooden bowl, cut up carrots, broccoli, set out bowls of tomatoes, olives, hummus—it was as much as she could do. She was looking forward to the dinner tonight. Jack would grill the meat. She needed to shower and change her clothes.

The warm water rushed over her tight shoulders and she sighed—oh, the strangeness of her children, to feel that sudden wall, to not know them—despite the care she took not to hurt them. She whipped shampoo into her scalp, rinsed, poured the conditioner on her hand, and ran her fingers through her hair. If anything happened to Tyler, she would be blamed, but how *was* she at fault?

She scrubbed her body as if five tiny mice were at work inside her washcloth. She was clean now. She dried herself in a big white towel and massaged lotion into her feet and legs, her breasts, neck, and face. She opened her cosmetics drawer: face powdered, cheeks blushed, lips painted light peach, eyelashes outlined. She ran a brush through her long gray hair and left it to dry.

She stood before the mirror; her clothes fell in elegant lines over her tall, slim frame; her feet were supple and still beautiful. She slid them into flats and added a string of pearls. Dinner was an occasion, especially now when no one dressed for anything.

After the banter by the grill, the finger foods dipped and eaten, after Jack put the steaks on and James took them off, after the cell phones were silenced (at last) when sunlight slanted through the hours and the house darkened enough to turn on a few lamps, she called them in. James in his yellow cotton shirt with navy stripes, in his jeans and sandals, was still a boy.

He floated away from his legs as he walked, as if he were made of seaweed, her tall child. Jenny followed in a light shift dress the color of blue hibiscus, and Sarah saw the smooth column of neck, the dancing dark ponytail, the arc of her gold earring as she turned.

Jack came last, carrying the plate of steaks, the skin stretched thin over his forehead in concentration, his face a terrain of small caves cut by half lines, half circles, as if he were halfway between the fullness of his life and its ending, which Sarah supposed, was quite possibly true.

She called up the staircase for Tyler, who bounced down in shorts, flip-flops, and a t-shirt. "Change into a dress," Sarah began.

"Oh, let her be," Jenny countered.

They moved under two sets of arches from the deck to the kitchen to the dining room, into an interior lit by tall candles, and when they sat, ladies first, the light in their eyes was bright with anticipation. Tyler had her cell phone at her place (it was a rule not to have it at the table), but Sarah said nothing, not wanting to spoil the dinner.

She served cold gazpacho in small, translucent bowls and wondered what they would talk about tonight. And

62

then, seeing James exchange a smile with her, she heard the conversation bubble up and lull and rise again against the ambient noise of the crickets outside. Sarah ate slowly and watched the scene, as if they, her own family, were from another time and culture.

The four adults ladled their soup away from the front of their bowls; the little oars dipped and skimmed the sides of their bowls. Her tribe ate slowly, their motions synchronized with small talk. Yet, she thought, we are all here to find our place at the table, to belong. But they were laughing now, and she laughed, too, and Jack coughed once, softly, and touched his lips with his napkin.

The steak was tender, grilled just right, and Sarah ate slowly, cutting a small piece, placing her knife across the plate, spearing the sliver of meat with her fork, hand in her lap, her back straight, her head inclined, listening as she chewed.

"I heard about it online, a new remedy. It's delicate pale green, and did you know it contains an antiviral?" What were they talking about? It was too late to ask. In any case, it was surely a false hope.

James, a newly minted architect working online at odd hours, was talking about 'underground heating pumps and underground wires, too' for a new housing complex design. But, he admitted, he did not know when it might get built, or how long he might be able to work with no real building happening.

"Underground wires, huh? I used to dream about the electric wires that looped out behind this house being cut by a sinister hand," Jack said. Sarah wondered if this explained the sudden losses of electricity, those scurried searches for flashlights and warnings not to open the refrigerator or everything would be spoiled.

She should be having a wonderful evening but she could not concentrate, and her hearing lagged, as if delayed a beat or two.

"He solved the Rubik's cube just like that...the loan, yeah, it was a foolish gamble, but what else could he have done...that was his problem, wasn't it...maybe that's the point...no, it's not so apparent to me...St. Patrick wasn't Irish after all, did you know that...no, not a good bargain, it's just a ruse to get you to...it happened twice and that's one time too many...they reopened with all these measures in place...I took on a new shift today; they need nurses desperately."

Sarah swallowed and spoke, "You took on what new shift?" Jenny looked at James; he glanced back, a glance that said, 'I can't believe you have not told her.'

"Yes, there's a world out there beyond this house where people are sick and dying. I didn't expect to be asked, but now I am to work one shift at the weekend in the Covid unit." James ducked his head and Tyler looked up from her phone.

"Is there anything else I should know? You do realize you are exposing all of us?" Sarah asked, keeping her voice steady.

"Mom, it is not this huge risk you make it out to be. We are all in PPE, all in N-95 masks, and the rooms are ventilated anyway. Everyone complies, even the cleaning staff. And I change clothes and shower when I come from the hospital as it is. There is no real danger."

"No danger, you must be kidding," Sarah said.

Jenny was silent; the silence descended over them all, and even the cutlery went silent. Sarah rose to clear the table. A knife clattered to the floor and Jenny picked it up, followed Sarah into the kitchen. Sarah filled the dishwasher as Jenny hovered.

"Mom, Mom, please don't. Mom, I'm sorry I didn't tell you before I said yes, but I didn't know you'd be this upset."

Sarah stacked the glasses in rows in the top section, her back to her daughter.

"Mom, listen, I felt I had to do this. The weekend nurses are all exhausted from this. I could help a little. I know it wasn't right to keep it from you."

Sarah turned. "And why is that?"

"Because I knew it would hurt you."

"Hurt me. This does not hurt me, Jenny. I do not interfere with your decisions." Sarah's eyes brimmed and she turned away.

She went upstairs, leaving them to enjoy the strudel without her. The day that began so long ago with the promise of their favorite dessert had unraveled to this, and she was damned if she'd go down to say goodnight. Eventually, she heard footsteps coming up the stairs. Jack sat on the edge of the bed and took off his jacket, his shirt; his shoes fell to the floor one by one.

"Well?" She asked, sitting up behind her book.

"So, we know now that she's taking another shift," he said.

Sarah went back to her reading. She read the same sentence over and over, as if she could make it speak to her through her bitterness: *I wonder what people are most afraid of? A new step, their own new word, that's what they're most afraid of.* This sentence did not make any sense to her.

Jack brushed his teeth in the bathroom with the door open, ran water, and trundled back to bed in his bare feet, scuffling the carpet, whistling. How could he whistle? Was he pleased, or amused? Sarah threw off the covers and went to the window. She looked into the backyard, and out there, somewhere beyond the horizon of thinking and fuming, her tears came.

She leaned against the sill, and then there was Jack, the polished cotton expanse of his pajamas and chest; she turned and leaned against him.

"Are they alright?" she asked. Jack hesitated long enough for her to raise her head and look at him.

"He noticed you'd gotten rid of his Christmas sweater, the one you gave him last year, and he wasn't a bit pleased about it."

She ducked her head, smiled despite herself.

But it was difficult to sleep. Moments of consciousness flickered in and out in a long drift, carrying strange images and ideas in their wake: she looked down at a river and saw birds flying across the wide shimmering water; she saw James dressed in whites and carrying a tennis racket; she reached out for a book, *Ryan's Gold.*

The wind knocked a twig against the window and, swimming back through the coarse net of the senses, Sarah awakened. Her tongue was heavy in her mouth, her hairline damp with sweat. She kept her eyes closed to revisit her dream. She saw the dream unfold again in cinematic clarity.

A small girl wearing a smocked summer dress stood next to a woman at the kitchen sink. Sarah followed the

66

child's gaze as she looked up. The woman had a raven's head, and in her beak was a nugget of gold. The child reached up to her, holding out a box of Crackerjacks, as if to appease her.

Sarah pulled herself up on the pillow, pushing off the covers. It was not unusual to wake several times at night with a hot flash, and a few minutes later, she'd cover herself and sleep again. But tonight, she was sweltering. The season of bleeding had ended; her children grown, gone, and returned home unnaturally, with their own children.

She remembered their little ears in the bath and their cries against baby shampoo in their eyes, as though *she* were in there, stinging. They had no awareness of their own eyes blinking connected to this pain. She alone was responsible. It had been such a relief to get each child into bed, their soft breaths going in the night, hands around some bit of blanket, holding to life.

You think you can see it all coming and move your body in the way to protect them. You think nothing will be marred or damaged or lost forever.

Jack was snoring peaceably. Men, it seemed to her, did not consider such things.

Irritated, sad, and now wide awake, Sarah slid out of bed and put on her cotton robe and slippers. She was thirsty. She went down the stairs and stood in front of the open refrigerator in the dark kitchen, its light nearly too bright to focus. She poured a little cranberry juice into a glass, filled it up with water from the faucet, and drank deeply.

She spotted her cell phone on the counter, looked at her watch and saw that it was 3am. She would call Maggie. She and Maggie had been through it all together—Maggie's divorce and Sarah's struggle with anorexia, though she still hated that word.

Sarah searched for Maggie's name, and when she answered, Maggie's voice was instantly alert. "What's wrong? Is anyone sick?" she asked.

"No, no, not that," and it all tumbled out, the small disasters of the day. Among the things Sarah loved in Maggie was Maggie's calm, her invariable 'we'll get through this' approach to life's difficulties, large and small. But Maggie was no fool, and once Sarah had unburdened herself, Maggie would edge her friend to the heart of the matter with keen questions.

"Why did you want to suddenly give away Jenny's dungarees?"

"Oh, I don't know." Sarah inhaled deeply and added, "And I took the sweater I gave to James, too." Sarah slumped over the counter, crying softly.

"Well, what came over you?" Maggie asked.

Sarah sniffed and leaned her elbows on the cool countertop. "The whole day has been strange from the moment I turned my attention away from Jenny to making my strudel…and for what, for what? All day long, I've given things or taken things to give them away."

Maggie interjected, "What were the things meant to do?"

"To do? I just wanted to be seen, to be appreciated, not always and only a mother, and at the same time, no longer a mother and therefore, no one at all. I have no authority so I'm nothing to Tyler, my one grandchild, and…" she trailed off.

"But you are, you are someone to me," Maggie countered.

Sarah sighed. "Yes, I suppose that's true." Maggie was quiet, waiting. "Jenny's going to work a weekend shift on a Covid unit. She didn't even tell me."

"Oh," Maggie said.

"I was so upset with her when we are all being so careful."

"They are living in your house and this virus is deadly. You had every right to be angry and upset!"

Sarah laughed. "Yeah, suppose, oh I can't even think it."

Sarah heard a car go by and turn the corner. She felt calmer, amazingly much calmer. What had seemed unthinkable was simply that she could do little to nothing to protect her family, and her anger had seemed suddenly personal and petty against what they were all facing: the possibility of dying and no way out of the situation that she could see.

After she hung up with Maggie, she rinsed her glass at the sink. The little girl in her dream had a look of pure fear. A mother was a domestic God, benevolent perhaps, also heedlessly powerful? The woman had gold in her mouth, no, gold in her beak. The child's offering of the Crackerjack box seemed terribly sad, and it now seemed to Sarah a kind of fool's gold. Something fearful and false was being exchanged between them.

But she could not, for the life of her, connect herself as a mother with a bird of prey, and she felt sick to think of a mother and the child like that.

To the Nth Degree

We cannot solve our problems with the same thinking we used when we created them.

—Albert Einstein

White clouds with swollen charcoal underbellies drifted above her on a light wind. Nora passed the empty soccer fields and cricket fields in the Phoenix Park in Dublin, where she walked twice daily. A young man sat alone on one of the benches that lined the walk, reading. Well, she supposed, it was still alright to read outside. An old man leaned on the long red handle of his rake studying the sky.

The trees had already begun to shed their leaves in early October. The sun broke through the clouds and shone on the vibrant green lawns. It was strange to be living in the city where she was born, where the light, the air, the sounds assembled themselves as experiences of origins.

Nora had a Fellowship at Trinity College. It reopened on the 28 of September with the plan that laboratories and tutorials would take place on campus and lectures online. In practice, going onto campus remained largely optional.

The Science Gallery, where she was to work on a special program on mathematics and infinity for young people, had provided her an office and computer, but Nora saw no sense in going into an almost empty office building every day.

The Trinity academic year was divided in the same manner as Oxford: Michaelmas went from October to December, Hilary from January to early March, and the

Trinity term from late March to May. She rolled the sounds of these words around in her mouth, savoring them. Maybe it would be different by January.

Nora worked via Zoom; it made little difference where she was as she joined her weekly meeting. Her project proposal had paired her with a poet: 'Two approaches to infinity: mathematics and poetry.' Cian, the Kerry-based poet from Ballyferriter, as it turned out, knew almost nothing about math. That was fine; she'd have to explain everything to him, a good way to build her ideas with secondary school students in mind.

Nora looked forward to their meetings, set for 11am on Wednesdays. Zoom was easy enough. She liked meeting in her cozy slippers, cup of tea at her side. After the usual weather report from the East and West coasts of the island, they got to work. Cian, blue-eyed with black hair, was still a young man. She enjoyed his descriptions of mist and rain, and of surfing in the Atlantic in a wetsuit, no matter the weather.

"Alright," she began, taking a sip of hot tea. "To move around in this question of infinity, I thought we'd begin today with the idea of a proof."

"Is a proof a calculation?" Cian asked.

"Not really. It's a demonstration. It shows you a logic, built from abstract ideas and written in the most elegant terms. Its origin is a theorem, and you can have many proofs from a single theorem."

"Go on, give us an example."

"Let's take a theorem." She reached for a pad of paper and spoke as she wrote: "The nth function is $f_n + 1/f_n$, where f_n is the nth Fibonacci number. This is very basic."

"To you, it is. What is a Fib, you know, one of those numbers?"

"It's a sequence in which every number is the sum of the two preceding it, and it's a remarkable sequence in mathematics. These sequences are hidden in growth processes—like the number of spirals and counterspirals in sunflower heads."

"Ah, Sunflower, weary of time...Your man Blake was onto the same idea." Cian grinned. He liked making connections to poetry.

Nora frowned, not wishing to be sidetracked.

Cian continued: "Come here to me. I've not quite got this number sequence."

"Follow the pattern. Don't fight it: 1, 1, 2, 3, 5, 8, what comes next?"

"I've absolutely no idea."

"Five plus 8 equals?"

"Thirteen, as in *Thirteen Ways of Looking at a Blackbird*. You just add the previous two numbers, that's it?"

Nora nodded. "There are these beautiful connections, Cian, between the Fibonacci numbers and ϕ, phi, starting with a simple expression of an infinite formula: the square of the square root of 2 plus the square root of 2, going on and on...if you take this infinity and divide it by 8, you'll get π, pi, approximately 3.14159...the circumference of a circle."

"I don't get it. Can you share your screen?" Cian asked.

"How do I do that?" Nora asked him.

"Never mind. I'm not sure this will connect with poetry for me. Can you tell me about mathematics any other way?"

"I've been thinking in numbers for a very, very long time. I don't know any other way."

"Em…try this. Just pull out some words, some phrases connected with some of the main concepts in mathematics, physics, whatever—words that reverberate with the idea of infinity for you."

"Just words? No explanations?"

Cian nodded and reached for his pen, waiting in the face of Nora's consternation.

"I was going to explain eventually: The Golden triangle, Universal uniqueness, the Infinite Staircase, Folding conics. You really don't want to know what any of this means?"

"No. This is grand. What are conics? Cones?"

"Yes, there's a whole mathematics of cones in relation to ellipses and the discovery of…"

"Janey Mack! Please don't. I don't want it spelled out to the nth degree."

"But then we are each going to be in prison with our own language, unable to convey what is most simple, what is most compelling and interesting to us."

"Yes. Silence is deafening and words whirl around us. We are alone. That's where poetry begins."

Nora sat back. She didn't know whether to cry or to laugh. She'd wanted to go on, to tell Cian, rehearsing again to herself the known territories of her mind, built on the ideas of others over centuries: conics, orbits, how Kepler saw it, God's imperfect creation, heretical, what was then the edge of the un-imaginable.

She was prepared to get to Einstein eventually, light as a constant in the universe, all of relativity that followed, the edge of worlds and dimensions beyond the visible. Was this not poetry too?

"Nora?"

Cian tilted his head and spoke softly, looking at her intently. "I do want to understand your mathematics, as far as that is possible for me, which is just a little sliver of it. Go on, write up those proofs, email them to me and show me how they work. But what interests me is an empty place in my mind where truth is a tiny speck seeking just a few words for what eludes me."

Nora walked down Oxmantown Road to get fresh milk, a relief to be out walking in the sudden sunshine with only her thoughts. She told herself she should have begun with numbers, integers, fractions along a line, negative numbers, and worked her way toward introducing imaginary numbers. A poet would surely want to understand imaginary numbers.

Here was a pair of young women walking in front of her and crossing her path in their torn jeans, their coats open to the air, walking in a careless rhythm, earbuds of music so loud that she could discern a distant tinny bass. Here was an older woman in a mask with a large handbag and walking quickly. Quite a few people were out walking by noon. All they could do was walk, after all.

The Dublin Nora's father and grandfather knew well had been a Dublin of many bicycles and few cars, a city where horses delivered coal and milk and the spark of excitement came from the loose pig chased and cornered, put on a rope halter, while women stopped their prams and looked on. It was not a time in Nora's memory, although she recalled the occasional horse and trap rounding a corner. There were few cars now.

How would she explain numbers to Cian? The idea of square roots of negative numbers was at first, for those sixteenth and 17th century mathematicians, an act of conjuring. They called them 'noetic radicals,' those impossible numbers that made it possible to think daringly, to go out on an edge. What could be more exciting than that?

Nora put her milk in her small refrigerator, then sat at her kitchen table with her tuna salad sandwich and apple cut into pieces sprinkled with cinnamon. She ate slowly. Lines, vectors, conics, and the fluting of space/time in a fourth dimension tore her from the present into a fast-paced, badly edited film in which Cian was dazzled and inspired by her sketches and words.

Children's voices from the school two streets away came to her through an open window and brought back the smallness of her hand in her father's hand. Words like 'conkers' and 'craic' came to her like numbers plucked from the air, conjured a park and a game she'd played with hard chestnuts.

Words gathered images, arranging sequences so that Nora no longer saw the sink as she washed her few dishes. She decided to go out; the rain was beginning to fall in a light drizzle. She'd go to Smithfield for fresh fruit, a short walk. She put on her black N-95 mask and entered The Good Food Market, amazed by its many aisles and numerous displays.

Smithfield had once been an open-air fruit and vegetable market, and on every first Sunday of the month, a raucous horse fair. Now modern apartments, luxury food shops, and tall streetlights with great panels in the shape of wings made a very different tableau. The square and surrounding streets were alive with people seeking lunch or perhaps seeking diversion.

Nora remembered a milling sea of boys and men here, horses being groomed, and one old, weary, dirty brown pony she'd wanted to buy with five shillings she'd saved in a jar. There was some blindness to this objective, only made evident by her blind father's refusal to permit it. Suddenly, Nora was in tears. The memory stung; something that had been marred was still in her, waiting for this sudden moment. She walked up Manor Street.

The wide street with parallel footpaths became world lines that went on and on into infinity. She longed for some version of mathematics that could explain this marred thing she'd met again in Smithfield.

Here were the old Norse street names: Olaf Place, Norseman Place, Thundercut Alley. Nora walked up Manor Place and along Oxmantown Road to number 13, with its red door. She turned the key to her temporary home, a rented two-story artisan's dwelling from another century with a tiny back garden.

The front window abutted the footpath and people walked by in the evenings with only net curtains to divide the life of the street from the intimacy of her sitting room fire. Identical houses and chimney pots ran the length of the street. She'd grown up on Murtagh Road, two streets away, more than four decades ago. Tired of thinking, seeking some interruption from her own mind, she went upstairs and crawled under the duvet for a nap.

Nora woke to the sound of her cell phone. She smiled as she read the message: 'Nora: *We are bees of the invisible.* That's Rilke's idea! I will call them (fabulously) Fabonacci numbers. Your words yield honey, after a buzzing kind of afternoon. What does *fn* mean, and for that matter, *n*? Do you know anything about black holes? Of course, you do. See you next Wednesday. Cian.'

Nora came down the stairs with fresh energy. Outside, the sun was shining again and flooded in through the kitchen window. She would go for a long walk in the park. She took a light jacket and headed up the North Circular Road to the Phoenix Park. She wound her way among walkers, runners, cyclists, skate boarders, and a gaggle of children going to the Zoological Gardens. People were once again out in the park at this hour.

Nora arrived at the Victorian Tea Rooms, a small octagonal shaped building built in 1895 as a refreshment kiosk. It was open. The trees, flooded in sunlight, were just beginning to thin in October. Nora scuffled through them to join the line at the serving window, careful to stay two meters distant. She loved this old landmark with its terracotta tiled roof surmounted by its copper ball.

A woman handed her a steaming cup and queried, "Are you having a nice holiday?" Nora's accent signaled to everyone that she was an 'American.' It crossed her mind to say, 'I was born here,' but she simply nodded and went with her cup and plate of scone to an empty table out among the leaves.

When she'd finished her treat, Nora continued up Chesterfield Avenue along a path by the side of the road apart from the traffic. She wandered over to a grove of trees and beyond the trees found a more beguiling path. It would be easier to explain a black hole than the expression *fn* to Cian. She would enjoy telling him that they were not holes at all, but something else, and that you couldn't see them, even with the most powerful instruments.

You could only look for the effects of a tremendous warping of space-time after the collapse and crushing of matter in a kind of gravity no one could even imagine. You could theorize the 'before,' and see the effects of the 'after,' but of the thing itself, you could know nothing. She could trace her life back to this place, this city, but it seemed her memories had never happened here.

She remembered being cold and wearing a navy-blue wool coat in downtown St. Louis. Looking into the shop windows, she used the point between her father's ear and collar in the reflecting glass as her compass. But no word would do for what had invaded her here before that time. She could not analyze, calculate, plot, or say anything of that.

The Phoenix Park is the largest urban park in Europe. Nora did not realize she was lost until she came upon the *Ordinance Survey* sign, a blue and white sign posted next to a drive with two pillars on either side. Looking at the buildings beyond the entrance, she thought that perhaps a map of the park might be useful.

She saw a man heading toward a single parked car and ventured to ask him if it might be possible to buy a map of the park. The man turned to look at her. He was no longer young but he had the kind of head one would wish to sculpt if one had such skill: full lips, squared jaw, and high forehead. His eyes were light brown and warm.

"We're closing up now, but certainly, we've all sorts of maps, and you can look at them tomorrow, buy any you like."

"The problem is that I'm lost," Nora said softly. "And I need one now."

Perhaps he saw that it had cost her something to say this. He put his mask on and Nora did likewise. He led her to the back door of his office building and brought her into his world of maps. Rather than simply handing her a map of the park, he saw her interest as she turned around, wide-eyed. He decided to offer a tour, show her how the old maps were once made.

He told her solemnly how most maps mangled the Irish place names with awkward English approximations. Then, with deft hands at a keyboard, he printed out a detailed map of the park in full color, neatly rolled it up and handed it to Nora, saying, "By the by, I'm Eugene O'Brien."

Nora held the map in her right hand and extended her left hand—no that was wrong, so she shifted the map to her left, laughing, before taking his hand and telling him her name.

When they came out, it was dark and rain was falling. The streetlights on Ordinance Survey Road each made a hazy halo of rain.

Eugene smiled and said, "It is fortunate that you now possess a map, but where are you going in the dark and the rain?"

There was something tender and amused in this, and Nora said, "Back to Stoneybatter, where I live."

"Oh, I have a house in Stoneybatter too, in Carnew Street. Would you like a spin?"

Nora hesitated.

"Look, I can open the windows; we can wear masks."

He opened the car door, took out a black umbrella and opened it over her head. The rain fell from the canopy onto his sleeve, and he waited.

"Of course, if you'd rather walk, you can take this brolly and bring it to me tomorrow here, or stop by later at number 7 Carnew, if that's easier…"

"No, I'm meeting my aunt tonight."

"You won't want to be late, then; hop aboard. Your feet will barely touch down before you are at your door."

She pulled her mask from her pocket and stepped in.

But her feet did touch down. She pushed them into her damp shoes and noticed herself elated in his presence. It was as though they had entered a pool of light, the park and city near, yet outside and far away, dissolving in the rain and dark, and it was hard to tell if she was under the surface of that pool, or just surfacing above it, into a new time.

She ached to make this last, to spend the entire night driving around with this stranger.

Nora turned on a lamp in the sitting room, sat in a soft chair, and untied her damp walking shoes. She still held the map and now she touched the rubber band Eugene had wound about it—as though this gesture might seal a connection to him, a man she was unlikely to ever see again. Immediately, as if in refusal of that possibility, she imagined returning to the Ordinance Survey offices.

But she was to meet her aunt in just twenty minutes. Nora changed into a thick woolen sweater, fresh warm socks, her raincoat, and waterproof boots, before walking two blocks to 'Plan B,' a restaurant in what was once a small grocery store. They had arranged tables and chairs outside under a canopy with heating columns for the diners' comfort. Well, almost comfort. Nora knew she would feel the cold.

She supposed the stooped woman with gray hair walking toward her must be her Aunt Maureen. Nora did not remember her mother's youngest sister. She rose and gave her a light kiss on her cheek, shy with this relation who reached out and caught Nora in an unexpectedly strong hug.

"Oh, child, look at you!" the older woman exclaimed, and Nora had to laugh at being the 'child.'

"May I call you Maureen?" she asked.

Her aunt smiled and nodded.

Maureen handed Nora a menu and looked up at her niece, blinking.

"When I last saw you, you were up the street here, outside the Manor Picture House, crying your eyes out about leaving Síog, not us, but your little black cat."

Nora didn't remember this.

A young server came to the table, offered her a taste of the wine, and stood waiting.

"How do you prepare your chicken?" Nora asked him.

"We take her out back, squat down, look her in her eye and say 'You're gonna die,' and then, well, you don't want to know all that." His face, impassive, broke into a grin and they all laughed.

Nora was continually taken by surprise with the wit everywhere in Dublin. She ordered a roasted breast with mash and asparagus.

Maureen worked her pasta slowly around her fork against the brace of her spoon. "I have returned recently, too, Nora, just three years ago. I moved to London when I was just twenty-one, worked in Lord and Taylor's selling hats, and then married an Englishman and had two children. When my Gerry died, I came back to Dublin, but coming back here, oh, I'm not 'home' here anymore than I was in all those years away."

Nora nodded. "Yes, I know; everywhere I go, people think I am American. And I am, I suppose. But I want to ask you about my mother, your family, all of it—whatever became of all of you."

Maureen took a sip of her wine. "You remember that we lived on Viking Place in a small cottage? Your mother would come to visit with you when you were a baby. Do you remember, Nora?"

Nora shook her head.

"Well, when we were growing up, there were nine of us, seven children and mam and da. Your mother, Nelly, was the eldest, and I was the youngest. When Nelly died of TB; it was the curse then that this Covid is today…"

Nora was stunned. "Are you sure it was TB? Not the flu."

"No, you had the flu and got well. Your mother died of TB a few months later." There was a door in Nora's mind she could not open to this possibility. She was sure her mother had died when Nora was sick.

Maureen went on, "Your mother could sing! Do you remember her singing?"

Nora bit her lip and nodded. "Yes, I remember that."

"Your grandfather was a cooper, a barrel maker, and he worked at the Guinness Brewery, as had his father before him. Coopers' measures had to be exact, or the barrels leaked—and your grandfather was a very exacting man. I suppose that's where you got your love of numbers."

Nora smiled to think of that.

Maureen smiled, too. "We were poor, yet not the poorest—we had enough to eat, usually soup, and bread and jam for our tea. We went to all the ceilis all around Dublin, went everywhere on our two bicycles. Almost all of us emigrated, Sean and Eoin and Cillian to Australia, only Mary and Dermot stayed. Your cousins, Jason and Gillian, are both grown now, living in London."

"I have British cousins?"

"No, to be sure, they remain Irish." Maureen took a bite of bread and laughed. "Tell me about yourself, what are *you* doing now?"

"I'm working on at the Science Gallery at Trinity on a project about infinity—with a poet."

"Are they open again?" Maureen asked.

"Yes, but no, not really, but I have a key and an office there. I have not seen anyone else there, except the security man. Anyway, the idea behind the project is to invite young people in high school, um, secondary school, to invite them into the world of physics through the arts. I meet the poet, Cian, once a week, on Zoom. I was trying to show him some simple equations today to get us started." Nora watched Maureen's face for signs of boredom.

"Why must you start with math?" she asked.

"Because you have to have numbers to think about infinity; it is a universal language, and once you learn some crucial ideas, you can begin to ask amazing questions about..." She paused to consider how to say it. "Well, about the origins of the universe! The problem is where to start, how to get young people hooked."

Maureen nodded. "You were always smart, Nora; I'm sure you'll discover a way. But where does the poetry come in?"

Nora waited to gather her thoughts. "Einstein once said, I think he was the one who said it, 'You can't solve a problem with the same kind of mind that created it.' So, the idea with these Science Gallery funded projects is to nurture a different kind of mind in the next generation."

When Nora got up to leave, Maureen gave her a packet of photographs. Once inside her house again, Nora could not get warm. The heating had been off during the day and all evening, and by now, the damp had penetrated the thick walls. It was colder still in the bathroom across from the kitchen with its outside wall.

Nora brushed her teeth, washed her face, came out and started up the stairs, then went back for her packet, and up and up the stairs slowly, peering into it. She turned on her electric blanket, put on her pajamas, added a sweater, and propped her pillows against the headboard. She laid the photos out on her duvet.

Here was her grandmother coming out of a door, light spilling around her against a dark hallway. Here was Maureen with Nelly in front of the Stoneybatter Post Office, match-box small, between Noel's Grocer and the Barber shop. Here was a child, oh that must be herself, sitting on the back of a bicycle loaded with baskets and bags holding onto a woman, surely Nelly, surely her mother.

As though time heaved open wide a gate in her mind, Nora remembered them: Annie Muldoon, the fishmonger, and Noel Lynch, the grocer, Billy Storey, the pig-raiser, and Sarah Murray, midwife and nurse. She remembered Pat Maylett, the sweet shop owner with his Honeybee sweets, BB toffees, Circus toffees, Sailor's chew, and two-penny-caps.

She saw the pigeons come clamoring for bread in the street, then rise from the ringing pavement as a horse turned a corner. She watched the mothers, in or beside doorways, teacups in hand, shouting behind them and raising one arm like a half parenthesis as the children swarmed under them into the clean, rain-chased air. She wore small leather-stiff shoes and had small hands with untidy fingernails.

She remembered getting lost going out for the morning bread for her mother. Which way? Was it down Red Cow Lane around by Norseman Place? She'd stopped to punch open a milk bottle and gulp it down, leaving a little ring of white in the bottom—before racing around a corner and vanishing, where?

She'd been a child on Murtagh Road, swinging on a rope from a lamppost. And before that she'd been a baby in the pram by the front window, out for air in her parked pram. She could have become any of them: Ellen Duffy or Mary Ockey or Molly Barker or Rena Cody. And here was her Síog, the cold coming off his fur, up into her lap. Ah, he's been by a fire by the smell from him.

The moon that rose over Euclid Avenue in St. Louis, Missouri when she was ten years old, had risen over the terraced roofs of Stoneybatter.

Nora awoke with her neck stiff, the lamp on, and the photographs scattered over the bed. She was fully awake now. She made her way downstairs. A cup of warm milk with a touch of vanilla, honey, and nutmeg would be just right. She took it up to bed.

She picked up a book, *The Physics of Black Hole Horizons*. She read: 'Inside a black hole gravity causes space to have infinite curvature so light doesn't stop. It continues along a straight path through infinitely curved space.' She'd explain to Cian, 'Think of the point of a cone. Right at the tip of the cone, the curvature is infinite.' But she never got to finish that thought because she went back to sleep again and into dreaming.

She saw her mother's headstone with the mark of infinity inscribed. Nora felt a sudden tug at her feet, a force from under the ground—a place from which light could never escape. The dream shifted suddenly. She lifted a little metal fish with a dorsal fin and moved it around a Monopoly Board marked out with the streets of Stoneybatter and the paths through the Phoenix Park. She counted forward and then backward, and set her fin down on Carnew Street.

Turning over, half awake, she smiled. Eugene was sleeping there.

A Sleight of Hand

Empty me of the bitterness and disappointment of being nothing but myself.

—Franz Wright

Neither dun sky nor spattered grit on snow could diminish Ben's pleasure as he walked from his car to Essalon for his coffee one Monday morning in early February 2021. It had been a long, cold, and isolated winter in Amherst. He was grateful for the earflaps on his cap and his black KN-95 face mask against the wind. He joined the line, keeping the required six feet apart.

A man with square, dark glasses, blonde hair falling sheepdog-style to the top of the frames, stood in line in front of Ben.

He turned around. "Professor Rubin!" He exclaimed, smiling a wry smile, "You've hardly changed at all."

Ben blinked and felt his eyebrows peak into the questioning shape of a roof.

"You remember me, the student in the back row? It's been ten years, but you couldn't forget me, even in a mask. Rick. Richard Snelling."

Ben nodded.

"All those lectures, on and on about Aristotle, came in handy. I went to CUNY, great philosophy program in metaphysics. I'm at Smith now: assistant professor."

Ben settled into the stranger's mistake; in these few exchanges, he became the mistaken man, Rubin, Professor of Philosophy—at which of the area's five colleges? He would displace his thoughts, his memories, even his field, for this appreciative man, an impromptu pretense that seemed, at least in this moment, his only place in the world. Ben decided to take things into his own hands.

"What was the topic of your dissertation?" he asked.

Rick spoke for some time about the metaphysics of truth. "Mostly it was on the work of Alain Badiou, on his 'truth procedure,' and I added a new spin to his critique of post-structuralism."

Unable to formulate a question, Ben made a sound, "Ermmm."

Rick got his coffee and Ben ordered a latte. He poured the latte into his thermos, destroying the swirled design on top, and headed to his car.

Ben drove to Hampshire College along Mill Valley Road, passing clapboard farmhouses and open fields, turned right on West Street, and took another right up the main drive into the campus. Proud of filling Rubin's shoes, shaking his head that he'd pulled it off not too badly, Ben wondered when Rick would realize his mistake.

The college now allowed professors to meet in person with students, as long as everyone wore masks. Among the older faculty, Ben was one of those rare ones who chose to go in, sick and tired of teaching via Zoom. This would be his first experience of seeing the students outside of that infernal matrix of boxed faces.

He heaved his briefcase from the back of the car. It was packed with six volumes, Proust in tow, and weighty enough to shift from hand to hand as he walked on the cleared and salted path.

Ben entered the classroom. The students looked up and waited for him to begin. It took him a few minutes to orient to their faces in masks. Then out came the six volumes of *In Search of Lost Time*, which Ben plonked down on his table.

"If you do not enjoy Proust, you won't read him, and if you don't read him, there is no sense at all in listening to me, or to anyone else, talk about him. This is the greatest novel ever written." He paused and no one said anything.

"Proust asks us reconsider many things: who you love, what you desire, how you experience time, and what it takes to become a reader, not only of Proust, but of yourself through Proust." Ben looked at his students, and they looked back at him as if there was nothing to lose. A young man sauntered in, shed his muffler and coat, took a seat.

"We begin at 9am sharp," Ben said.

A young woman with a purple streak in her hair raised her hand. "Are we really going to read *all* of it by May?" she asked, eyes wide.

Ben grinned. "Yes, but gradually, and not in sequence. And, by the end of the class, I hope you'll want to read it again." Ben knew that this was a lot to ask but he had asked it of Hampshire students before, and they'd done it. Some of his former students formed a new society, CPR for Continuing Proust Readers. They conducted a reading marathon of selections from *Search* on Proust's death day, November 18th, each year.

"Today, I'm going to read passages aloud, collecting a few sentences here and there, and pose questions to you." Since I anticipated that most of you would not bring your books, I made copies of the page we will study closely. This is from the second volume, *In the Shadow of Young Girls in Flower*," he finished as he dispersed copies.

He read: "Every now and then, when our little train stopped at one or other of the halts on the Balbec line, I was struck by the strangeness of their names—Incarville, Marcouville, Doville, Pont-à-Couleuvre, Arambouville…

"And in the dismal litany of these names, which were full of sand and salt and too much breezy space, with the startling syllable *ville* shrilling about them like a seabird, there was nothing to call to mind names like Roussainville or Martinville which, because I had heard them often said so often by my great-aunt, over dinner table in the parlor, had taken on a subdued patina of charm, an essence perhaps compounded of the taste of jam, the aroma of the wood-fire, the smell of the paper in a book by Bergotte and the color of the free-stone house opposite, and which to this day, when they travel up like gas bubbles from the depths of memory, retain their full specific virtue, though they have to traverse one after the other the many different layers of other mediums before reaching the surface."

Ben scanned the class of students, choosing one in the back row.

"Okay, Joseph, can you tell us what is going on in this passage?" Joseph sat up, blinked.

"Well, Proust is on a train, going through these towns, and he's thinking. Yeah, he's thinking about what the towns remind him of, and remembering being by the ocean and some things about being with his aunt."

"Yes, all that!" Ben confirmed. "And this is a good time for me to remind you that while Proust uses "I" to narrate, this is a character who is not Proust. Marcel is the protagonist of this novel, and though he shares a first name with Proust, he isn't Proust—he is a fiction. Now, Rebecca, can you build on Joseph's description and tell us what precisely triggers Marcel's memory of being with his aunt?"

"It's the sound of the names of the places, the repetition of 'ville' and then he thinks of her saying the names."

Ben interjected, "Ding, ding! Read more closely; he says, 'there was nothing to call to mind names like Roussainville or Martinville'..." Rebecca bent over the page, twirled her hair.

"It's confusing because the 'ville' does repeat, but it's just a litany. It's kind of like, like when you take a word and say it over and over and it loses its meaning...and then something else pops into your head."

Ben nodded. "Well done! And what pops into his mind?"

"His aunt?"

"Yes, but be precise."

"Then, the way she says those words."

Ben scanned the class. "Robert, what happens within Marcel as he remembers the quality of her voice?" The young man ducked his head.

"This is my first English class in college; can you come back to me later please?"

"No, you can do this. Just look at what he says."

"But the problem is that he says too much all at the same time."

"Yes! You have, in your first reading, put your finger on what is crucial in reading Proust—he constructs passages, and even single sentences, in which he says too much all at the same time. To read Proust, you must go slowly, gathering the threads with a wide-ranging attention. Read again, Robert, what does Marcel remember here?"

"He remembers the dinner table and the names get mixed up with other things: the jam, wood-fire, the book by Bergotte, and the house across the street. But that's not what he's really trying to say, only a part of it."

"You are a sharp reader!" Ben exclaimed. "Can anyone tell me just what Marcel is trying to say?" Four hands flew up. Ben chose a student he'd had in another class who was usually quiet: "Molly."

"The weird thing is that he says, 'There is nothing' to call to his mind the names his aunt was saying, and then he remembers all these things as if they are more real than the train."

"Yes, that's it. Proust does this all the time: he creates something veiled, or even absent, and then, in that gap, he makes something appear as more vivid, more real, than what is in front of Marcel."

Ben moved around to the front of the table and leaned against it. "This novel, and it is a novel, not a memoir, opens with an allusion to time, 'For a long time, I went to bed early,' and it ends with the word time. It goes from 'Longtemps' to 'Temps' in three thousand or so pages. Proust is not just wandering about being verbose in all these pages. He's working with time.

"The title of the book is *In Search of Lost Time*. He creates the experience of his character comprised of the residues of the past and conjectures about the future—and lived time, ordinary experiences, trigger these two other times. Let's call them retrospective and anticipatory times. He seems to be saying that we live too early and too late.

Malcolm Bowie, whom we'll read later, calls these two times 'a time of anxiety and a time of desire.'

"There are certainly time-effects of reading Proust, and you have already discovered them. He creates sentences in which 'too much happens all at once' and, in this way, he makes time do strange things to you. Between now and Wednesday morning, see if you can figure out how he makes his sentences work. What do all those subordinate clauses DO to you? Does everyone know what a subordinate clause is?"

They nodded, if uncertainly, back at Ben.

"Then there's a second thing you discovered about reading Proust this morning. You must be precise. The small details yield up larger ideas and the larger ideas lead back to surprising additional details. And to get it, you must distribute your attention over the text you are reading because your attention must be dispersed to see what he is saying, so try not to just gloss over his words and think you know what he is saying."

Ben took off his glasses. "I want you to read to each other before our next class. As you are reading—write this down—as you are reading aloud, I want you to be guided by Proust's thinking as it emerges in his writing. He says, 'There is nothing that so alters the material quality of the voice as the presence of thought behind what is being said.'

"The 'presence of thought' is there in the text—his thought—but no one, even *you* as you are reading, will hear it, unless you carry it on your voice when you read. So, that's your mission."

The students began to shuffle papers and rise.

"Wait," Ben raised his voice. "Then…"(there's a groan). "Then you are each to choose one long sentence and write me two pages about what that sentence is *doing* to you as a reader to *say* what it speaks *to you*. I'll post this assignment on our website so you can remember what I'm asking."

"Can you post that quote about presence of thought, too?" Robert asked.

"Sure, happily. Remember 9am sharp." Ben smiled under his mask. He hoped his eyes smiled, too.

Ben was surprised to see that it had begun to snow while he had been teaching, and the sky looked full of snow. He wasn't worried; he had new snow tires and lived only a few miles away. A crow rose from the path and flew in front of him to other crows perched high in a tree.

Ben followed the trajectory of its flight and stumbled on an ice patch, waved his arms wildly to find his balance, and found himself lying face-up, a group gathering around him. He was fine, he told them, wincing. Anna, his colleague and friend, ducked her head in among the students, "Get up slowly, you daft old man!"

"I was just looking at that bird and somehow made a misalliance with the ice," he explained. She picked up his briefcase.

"The weight of this alone would unbalance any normal human being," she added.

The rest of the morning went by without mishap. Ben moved around among books, piles of papers, and student files in his office, pottering about with a mug of tea for the better part of an hour before his individual appointments began. Ben was resigned to staying in his mask for most of the day. On today's schedule were students working on independent studies and those in their final year writing a thesis.

The hours of the morning and early afternoon flew as the students came and went with their ideas and plans. At 2:30, he went out to the HACU (Humanities, Arts, and Cultural Studies) office and saw the lights had been turned off.

"The college is shutting down now—you better get going while going is possible," Marge advised as she closed the door.

Ben shook his head. "Really, is it all that bad?"

"Yes, indeed—we are getting about a foot by 5pm."

"Are you alright for getting home?" he asked, knowing that she lived in one of the hill towns to the North of Amherst.

"I've got the Jeep, and that thing will take me anywhere."

Ben drove carefully. Carl had gone into Boston for a meeting but should be home by around 4pm. Ben rang his cell phone but only got Carl's voicemail. Often, while driving, Carl turned the music up full blast and didn't even hear the cell. Ben was not worried. He left a message that he was going out on his snowshoes and would have his cell with him.

Then he changed clothes, first a layer of thermals, building up to wool and fleece before pulling on his puffy down jacket. Next came his boots, laced secure, and his hat with the earflaps and insulated gloves. On the side porch, he strapped on his snowshoes, grabbed his poles, and slung on his small backpack with energy bars and a pair of extra socks.

He set off down a path that started behind the house, meandered back through woods to a meadow, and beyond the wide meadow to more woods. Ben adopted the slightly slower gait of snowshoeing as he floated out over the freshly falling snow, poles guiding him like long oars. The snow, falling fast and thick between the trees ahead, made them fade in and out, like mirages.

Ben whistled to see if any bird might reply, then tried out a whole series of warbles, but the birds were hunkered down in their nests and bushes for the duration of the storm. He came to a little downward slope and pushed his heel crampons into the snow and walked down easily.

In the distance he saw his favorite pine grove, always a place of peace and rest. Squinting into the trees, he noticed a figure sitting on the ground, someone small. As he drew nearer, Ben saw it was a child wearing a red cap. He rushed now, arms pumping, to see if the child was sleeping, or, for that matter, alive.

In just a minute, he saw the red cap snagged on pine boughs, laden with snow, a blanket of snow over a mound like a seated figure sculpted entirely by accident. Someone must have lost a cap and perched it there before this snowfall. Relieved, Ben sat on a fallen log, and took a bite from his protein bar.

When he was a child of eight and his brother six, they'd made a snow child, dressed it in their old clothes, put on a cap, coat, old boots. Their child sat on the ground, muffled to its eyes, leaning against the school building, and when the janitor found it, he thought a child had died of exposure in the night.

The principal had been furious, had called a school assembly and questions were raised about who had created the snow child. And though neither Ben nor his brother spoke up, some of the children knew who'd made it and identified the brothers. The two brothers had been spanked with a paddle. They expected to be chastised and punished again at home, but their mother gave them hot cocoa, smiled at the prank, and never told their father.

Ben came to another, steeper hill, and herringboned his way down. He stopped at the edge of a field, looked out and saw a swatch of the land through a gust of wind, but the snow was so thick that he felt walled out of the field itself, lost somewhere underneath, unrecognizable. He turned to go back to the house, wondering if Carl might be there, waiting.

But Carl had not returned. It was 5pm. The snow would have slowed traffic on the Pike. Ben checked the phone: no messages. He tried Carl's cell phone and couldn't get him.

Ben brought wood up from the basement, stacked it into the wicker basket, and started a fire in the wood stove with a couple of fat sticks arranged over wood blocks. The flame caught and spread. He added two stout logs, opened the draft fully, and closed the glass door. He took off his leather gloves and put them on the basket.

Ordinarily, at this moment, he would sit and enjoy the fire before working on their dinner. He went into the kitchen, dislodged frozen hake from the freezer and put the fish in a casserole dish of cold water. He went back to the basement to the wooden vegetable bin made by his neighbor, Fred, an old man now who had a little workshop down the road where he turned out all sorts of things from toys to carved birds and birdhouses to pieces of furniture, including, famously, his vegetable bins.

In the Pioneer Valley, many people had a share or half of a share in one of the local farms, and canned or saved vegetables. Ben returned to the kitchen with carrots, parsnips, anise, beets, and potatoes. He chopped steadily, lined up the vegetables on a battered baking tray, and brushed them with olive oil, adding four sprigs of rosemary. He popped them into the oven and set the timer, but he would wait until Carl returned to broil the fish.

It was the timer that woke Ben from his nap in the chair by the fire. He removed the vegetables. Placing the baking sheet on the top of the stove, he glanced up the kitchen clock and saw that it was 6pm. A jolt of acid cut into his stomach, more fear than hunger. He tried Carl's cell again: still no answer.

Why did he take a cell phone with him if he didn't use it? Where was he? He could be very near, making his way over backroads, or still out on the Pike. Ben looked out the window. The snow had stopped. If it had stopped here, surely it had stopped where Carl was driving. Jimmy had come and cleared the driveway while Ben was sleeping, but the road plows had blocked the top again.

He would go out and shovel; it would give him something to do. He put his own cell phone in his coat pocket, just in case, and pulled on his gloves and cap.

This snow was fresh and light. Ben cleared a path from the garage to the house in a few easy swipes of his shovel. Snow covered the cherry trees. Above them, the moon was coming up bright and full, casting intricate shadows on the snow in the front yard. Ben crunched up to the top of the drive where the snow was heavier, laced with sand and salt, and he worked more slowly, scraping down to the tarmacadam before moving to the next part of the embankment.

Three houses away, Fred was shoveling out, too. Their shovels echoed back and forth in the cold evening, as though in conversation. Ben would invite the old man to dinner and they could play cards. His company would distract Ben.

An hour's passing found the two men at the table, hats and gloves drying on the stone slab in front of the stove. They'd had their fill of hake and vegetables and cold beer. Ben had put aside a plate for Carl to be microwaved at some indeterminate time. He tried to concentrate on playing 'Brown's Bene,' a game where the wild card, a card that could be used to replace any card in a lay-down, kept changing with each hand.

Ben retained a slim lead in points that Fred calculated after each hand for most of the game, but in the end, it was Fred who won. There was no money at stake here, only Ben's pride in a game played well, and he had not been at his best. Imposed over how many aces were in the pick-up deck was an image of Carl freezing in a snowbank at the side of the road.

Ben brushed off this image but he couldn't keep track of the cards. He didn't say anything of what he imagined to Fred, but the old man began his card tricks, as if to distract Ben.

Fred started with 'Here, you shuffle the deck,' as if this made the trick open and transparent, which was never the case. Fred demonstrated his 'easy tricks' first: 'Find the Card,' 'Street Magic,' and 'Follow the King.' Ben selected cards, put them into the deck, and found them again as Fred predicted, and he could not discern what Fred was doing.

It was as if Fred could see through the hidden cards, could pluck some unknown card from thin air. In these moments, he seemed to force Ben to become the spectator to a procedure that had been explained and agreed upon, while he marked him out as a victim to a sleight of hand that remained wholly enigmatic. Ben found the tricks maddening and engrossing.

At 9pm, when Carl finally walked in the kitchen door, Ben was no longer waiting for him.

Ben retreated to the silence of his study, leaving Carl to heat his food and eat alone. Scrolling through his emails, deleting most, then answering one student after the other, Ben's fingers hit the keyboard as though he were drumming; if he typed fast enough, the letters forming could screen out Carl's presence in the house. The time of waiting was over.

He'd had a day filled with things he ordinarily loved: his Essalon coffee, Proust on the first day back on campus, snowshoeing, shoveling out under a full moon, and then the evening with Fred, the warm food, cold beer, and cards. And yet, the day had begun uneasily.

He'd been mistaken and made a useless sacrifice in becoming the man Rubin; he'd followed the flight of a bird and fallen; he'd felt the rhythm of walking out on his snowshoes, floating up and away from the mistakes of the day; then he'd mistaken a mound of snow for a child and remembered another snow child, and the paddling, and the warm hot cocoa, no comfort at all, as though he gotten away with something too easily.

He could imagine the janitor's horror, his fury.

Ben read an email about a grant application three times, then moved it into a desktop file. Carl was at the door.

"Are you coming up?"

"Hmm...later."

"Listen, I'm sorry I didn't call you. I forgot to charge the cell phone last night, and the Pike, well, it was too dangerous to get off looking for a pay phone that was probably no longer at any of the stops anyway. None of the ramps were getting plowed."

Ben did not answer but kept on with his typing.

It had been a brief and silent skirmish and he'd won. Carl was gone. Ben could hear him going up the stairs. Ben put the laptop on 'sleep' and turned to look over his notes for class the next morning. Carl reappeared in the doorway.

"I'm going to the Hampton Inn tonight," he announced.

Ben turned in his chair. "What? Don't be ridiculous. We are in Covid and you have only just been vaccinated. I'm the one who has every right to be angry tonight."

It was the wrong thing to say. Something ignited in Carl's face. "No, Ben, you are always angry, not just tonight. You worry about me as if I don't have any life or will of my own, as if...oh fuck, I don't even exist as myself, and then you're furious if I don't conform to your idea of me."

"What do you mean? I was worried, sure, but who wouldn't be when you are out there driving in a blizzard, no contact, for what, seven hours?"

"You never say your brother's name, Ben," Carl said. "Can't you say his name, for God's sake? Just say his name."

Ben sat in silence.

Carl turned away with a small bag, went down the hall, crossed another two rooms, and went out the kitchen door.

Ben sat still as he heard the car start, the garage door going up and then down. The house was silent now, save for the hum of the refrigerator, a log falling in the stove, and Ben went up to bed. Carl had never done such a thing. In fact, this was the quietest, shortest fight ever. He would surely be back in the morning, all apologies.

Ben put on his pajamas, washed his face, brushed his teeth, padded to his side of their bed, and kicked off his slippers. He sat. How strange to be here alone after waiting for Carl all day, and stranger still to think of Carl not far away, paying for a room—just to be alone.

Ben folded the cold covers around himself, as if he were a package that needed padding. It was chilly up here in this part of the old farmhouse. He closed his eyes and tried to sleep.

But Carl appeared and reappeared each time Ben drifted: Carl in the kitchen, pouring cups of coffee, making toast, flipping the radio on to WFCR, and bantering with Kari Njiiri or Terry Gross; Carl in a crisp white shirt, tie tucked under the apron front, scrambling eggs; Carl laying the table, putting down sectioned oranges on a plate between their two places; Carl whisking around the table doling out hot bacon.

His brother had never come up in their fights before. What did his brother have to do with anything that happened that day? None of it made sense.

Ben must have slept because he woke from a dream.

He was in a bare room, with only a writing table and a broken bicycle. He could write or repair the bike. He chose the bike. There was some error in the chaining. He kept trying to find the source, but as he handled the chain, his hands became cut and stained red. He continued to work on the bike, called a 'Martinville.'

Ben sat up in bed, pushed the covers aside, and pulled on a wool sweater. He turned the lamp on and looked at his hands. Martinville. What was that about? And then he knew. He had taught that passage from Proust how many times? Yet, he'd never heard his brother's name. And why was he fixing a bicycle when he wanted to write? His hands were stained, as if fixing the bike were tantamount to a murder. He thought of the snow child, and then Carl.

Is it possible to 'kill' someone by making him seem to be someone else?

He went downstairs, added a couple of logs to the fire, opened the draft and watched the fire take off. Carl would have turned his cell phone off. Ben opened his laptop and googled the phone number for the Hampton Inn. He asked for Carl's room, the phone rang, and Carl picked up.

"Martin," Ben said. "His name was Martin."

Of Sound Mind

What is the language using us for?
It uses us all and in its dark
Of dark actions selections differ.

—W. S. Graham

Aunt Ella Vator was tall, and carrying her tray ahead of John on the stairs, she looked taller still, for John was shorter and following; and as they went up, one with a tray of croissants, cheese, butter and strawberries, the other with a steaming cafetière, milk and sugar; two pairs of legs ascending to the upper terrace, their voices came down the echoing expanse of the winding stairwell like a distant music and fell away into the kitchen where Claire was boiling eggs that were also œufs.

An œuf and an egg rolled around in the pot like a distant music and fell away.

Claire's father had re-named his younger sister Ella Vator when she'd surpassed him in height six decades ago. The name had stuck; it became her. Claire had moved to the small village of Quillan in the Languedoc region in May 2021, a month ahead of her husband and aunt. They'd agreed it would be safer here than in Paris as the pandemic continued spreading in unpredictable waves. But moving the entire household was not simple.

Claire had wanted the time to paint before they arrived. There was a light working through her, and everything she saw formed a kind of improvisation with light. The urge to paint did not diminish with the arrival of her family.

The morning light was the best light. It was clear, brilliant light, no people about to interrupt seeing it; the café was not yet open, the streets were empty. The mosaic floors of an old church formed geometries in ochre, red, and magnolia. In a shabby, eloquent backstreet, Claire found a diminutive green door with a lion's head knocker, and next to it the number 3 painted in white on a blue porcelain square.

The quality of the light at this hour made impressions that stayed with her, as though certain things were pressed into her being, an intaglio of forms and colors beyond words. She had awoken at sunrise and opened the heavy wooden shutters to rooftops and mountains in the blue morning air.

Impossible to stay in bed, then wait for breakfast, the washing up, talking, deciding, waiting to organize—what would it be, a walk along the River Aude, or a visit to the outdoor market? Why wait? Quillan, at the foothills of the Pyrenees, shone at 5am on a summer's morning. Claire had crept out to paint before returning to the apartment for breakfast.

The eggs boiled away as she looked at the rooftop tiles across the narrow street from the kitchen window. Their interlocking U's climbed up and up in diminishing terra cotta rows. Claire wanted to paint the music of their ascending shapes.

"Hey," John called out from the doorway, "Claire, Claire, come on up. How long can it take to boil a couple of eggs?"

John did the dishes and tidied the apartment while Aunt Ella Vator had a shower and unpacked. Claire sat at the dining room table and studied her French phrase book. She had been slow to learn French while living in Paris for nearly two years, although she loved the accents of native speakers.

She bent over her little notebook to write out the words in English, then in French, then to spell out the phonetics of the French sounds. She wrote her thoughts—first as aids to memory, as commentaries on learning a language, and increasingly to decipher messages addressed to her through the phrase book.

She opened her notebook and wrote: '*En hiver*, in the winter, makes me shiver, the French goes *an nee-vehr*, a knee veers off from a leg, a sudden severing.' Claire looked down at her own knee, intact. '*Au printemps*, let's see temp is time, oh print time!' She thought of an old sign hanging over what she supposed was once a printing press. '*Imprimerie.*' It's time to print images.

She bent to write: 'Spring coming sounds like oh-pran-tahn. Close to won-ton? A fortune?'

Claire flipped through the book and found conversations, or at least the first lines of conversations. She learned how to say, 'Allow me to present myself. My name is. I am (choices of a student, a lawyer, a doctor, or a businessman). May I have this dance? Would you like a cigarette?' But it seemed to her extremely unlikely that she might say any of these things.

She turned the page and found 'Will you write to me?' Yes, she might ask someone that to see the words in print, go away and look them up, have time to ponder them before having to reply. She stretched in her chair, ready to get up and find her water bottle, but the phrase *Ne bougez pas* caught her eye, alongside the English translation 'Do not move.'

Suddenly, she could not move any part of her body. The frozenness lasted only a minute, and Claire wondered if it had to do with starting with the word for winter. But then, she was free to move again.

She put away the nasty little phrase book, gathered her water bottle, her sun hat, her canvas bag—for by now, they had decided it would be good to go to the open market in the morning before the heat of the day.

Aunt Ella Vator walked across the room wearing a light gray linen dress, open at the throat against her long neck. It made her graceful, willowy in her seventy-eight-year-old body. She smiled her crooked smile at Claire and tilted her white head to the left, and in that moment, Claire was six years old, meeting her aunt for the first time, swept up in a glance that spoke to her, alone, in the room.

John came out from the kitchen with a small basket, a dishtowel slung over his shoulder.

"No one will need you to dry dishes at the market, Monsieur," said Aunt Ella Vator gravely. John laughed and his laugh sounded and re-sounded in Aunt Ella Vator's softer laugh, and finally in Claire's chuckle, as if the joke had arrived a beat too late.

The three went down the winding stairs to the street. The market was arranged in an open square by the river, a joyful scene of red, blue, and orange canopies covering the stalls put out by farmers, fishmongers, cheese makers, and wine merchants. What joy to move about outdoors without a mask! The three joined the throng and bought apricots, asparagus, olives with garlic, almond, and mint centers, peaches flushed red and violet, and melons.

They selected three fresh trout, caught that very morning at the local mountain lake, the fisherman declared. They were alive when he lifted them from a tank of clear water, clattered each on the head with a wooden stick, weighed them, bagged them, and handed them over to Aunt Ella Vator.

John suggested they take a break in the shade of a café. They sat at one of the tables on the Promenade in the center of the village with their grandes crèmes. A light wind fanned the trees on either side of the avenue. At 10am in the morning, the day was already warm. The high blue sky would blaze heat by midday, and then the shutters would close until late afternoon.

"What are these trees?" Aunt Ella Vator wondered.

"Ah, those are plane trees," John said. "Planted as shade for horses pulling barges along the Midi Canal."

"Very kind to their horses," Aunt Ella Vator said.

"Yes, they were. You know those ancient cave paintings, the galloping horses? They're not that far from here."

"Oh, I'd love to see that, wouldn't you, Claire?" But Claire was studying a statue in the square and didn't hear her aunt.

On the way home, they stepped into the local Boulangerie to buy fresh bread and ask if Claire might paint Madame's hens. Claire returned with watercolors, paper and brushes, a jar of clean water, and a folding stool. Madame's husband, in a mask, ushered her through a narrow kitchen into a small back garden. Claire emerged from that short walk as from a cave into a flood of light, nearly blinding.

The hens came running as the man scattered invisible seeds and pecked at nothing. Claire set up her folding stool and paints. When she looked up, the hens were perched on a fence at the end of the garden. Its rails formed a lop-sided *M*, and the hens gripped the wood at an impossible slant. They stood upright, each looking off in a slightly different direction, as if enclosed on a packed bus.

They were mostly brown and orange, with bright yellow beaks, except for the smallest hen—she was pure white. A tree limb dappled the fence. The sun hit the hens and highlighted a piece of old twine binding the middle and third post in the shape of an *X*.

As Claire wet her brush, she wondered what it meant, this *M* and *X*. Aunt Ella Vator had a game with letters she'd taught to Claire and her sister when they were small. How did it go? '*F U N E M N X*?' It didn't make sense to Claire until her aunt translated, "Have you any ham and eggs?" Then the letters receded and the words jumped out. Claire painted the yellows first, leaving the paper white for the brightest light.

For the past several weeks, something strange had been happening; numbers and letters leaped out at her and did not make sense, and then suddenly, they did. A poster in the market this very morning intimated that she would have something to do with the Cathars, whoever they were. A statue of a woman stood in the village square and held a flame aloft.

Another statue of a woman stood in front of the church pointing to the sky and holding a flame, too. Suddenly,

Claire knew that the sky would catch fire. But when? There was a date: 17 Mars 1912. It was a code, and here before her in the fence was another part of the code.

With excitement, she turned her painting over and did the math. M was a thousand and X was ten; she subtracted those two numbers to get 990 and subtracted this from 2021, the current year, to arrive at 1031. But the numbers, she realized, should be grouped in pairs, because she'd seen a pair of statues.

She added the numbers of the mysterious date; Mars was March, so that was 03, and then 17, 19, and 12. It added up to the number 51. In fifty-one hours, the sky would burn. She remembered the number 3 next to the lion's head knocker; now it made sense—three messages. She had less than three days. Claire put her paints away and returned to the apartment.

The traditional siesta followed lunch. The apartment was quiet and dim with the shutters closed. Claire made cups of mint tea and stirred in honey. She climbed the stairs to Aunt Ella Vator's room. Her aunt was lying down on top of the bedclothes, propped up against a pillow. Her eyes were open, intent, as though studying something near her.

One shutter was closed, the other open with a lace curtain that moved in the breeze. As Claire stood in the doorway, she studied the folds of the gray linen dress, so like the folds of the old woman's face and neck, those little waves of loosened flesh, the shadows swimming under the chin. The high forehead was smooth with little creases down the middle, as though someone had rolled pastry dough in two directions.

Her aunt turned her head and spoke. Her face shifted—a garment hung too hastily on its hanger. For that moment, she was a foreign being to Claire, an impostor.

"Tea?" Claire offered. "It's mint."

She went downstairs to find John in a chair by the window. A crack in the shutter made a slice of light onto his book. John smiled at the tea. Claire sat at the dining room table across the room and spread out a map of the area, and there they were: *Sentier des Cathares*, walking paths through the Pyrenees the Cathars had used centuries ago.

She looked up. Everything was the same: the shutters, the lamp, the chairs, yet the whole place was imbued with a strangeness. John rose and took his cup to the kitchen. His neck seemed too long, as if structured partly as a giraffe, and his shoulders were a little too wide, too stiff. He turned and his face was deep in shadows, yet his eyes glowed. He struck a note of terror in Claire. "Do you mind if I turn the radio on low?" he asked.

While John dozed, Claire went to look at his book. As she'd hoped, it had a chapter on the Cathars. She sat in his chair, engrossed. The Cathars were a religious group who lived in villages all around the Pyrenees between the 11th and 13th centuries. The book showed photographs of their castles on rocky highlands, and their crosses, which Claire realized she'd seen on gates and in cemeteries on her walks.

The Cathars believed in two principles or forces at work in the universe—a good force that was transcendent love and an evil adversary based on power. The force of good could not have created human beings—since humans were endlessly destructive. Claire nodded. There was more. Their god had no name but was pure spirit. Humans were born to become pure spirit, though it might take many lifetimes to do so.

The Cathars were against the teachings and laws of the Catholic Church and called it 'the church of wolves.' Pope Innocent III sent a crusade against the Cathars. They were hunted deep into the Pyrenees and their mountaintop homes and driven off cliffs to their deaths.

Claire shut the book and closed her eyes. The radio was still on, very low. She got up to turn it off but stopped, her hand on the back of a chair. She heard a deep grazed voice, neither man nor woman.

At first, the voice reminded Claire of reading a letter and hearing the inflections of a known person speaking to you through the scrawl on the page. It was so direct, it was unnerving. But this voice, coming through the low static, suddenly moved and spoke into her ear, as if another person stepped up close beside her. "Ness pa?" it asked.

Claire could see the phrase in French, *N'est-ce pas?* Is it not? Is it not what? Is it not evil?

There was an evil breaking out everywhere, even in the bodies of John and Aunt Ella Vator.

In the late afternoon, the village re-awakened. It was like a second morning in the day. The light was soft now, and little swifts darted up from the eaves and trees and filled the sky. People went out to the shops and came home and began the slow ritual of making supper. With the shutters open, sounds traveled.

Somewhere below a group of children played a marching game, someone was laying out cutlery, a cupboard opened and closed, a motorbike went down the street, the flower shop bell rang, and next door a woman was playing Liszt. Claire paused at the cutting board with her onions to listen.

"It's the Transcendental Studies," John said.

'Transcend' stood out for Claire; it sounded a note of hope against the voices now telling her she was *useless, worthless.*

Aunt Ella Vator sat at the kitchen table, picking basil leaves from their stems, sipping a glass of white wine. Claire tried to concentrate on her task. Inside the rings of the onion, she could see faint letters forming, a fine tracing of a script. It read A R S; oh Cathars, Claire thought. *Disarm, disarmament is at hand*, a voice said suddenly. *Cut off an arm, a hand.* The red onion began to bleed.

Was someone tortured or murdered at this very moment for trying to write to her? Was Claire, unwittingly, herself the killer? She put her knife down and gathered the plates to set the table.

"Aren't you going to finish the onions?" John asked.

"No, not me," Claire answered simply.

John laughed as he took over the chopping. "Okay, alright."

Claire put a fresh cloth on the table. She laid out the place settings, four tiles in the center for the serving dishes, and put a vase of roses from the garden at the end of the table. She set out three wine glasses, three water glasses, and three napkins. She lit three candles in little blue glasses. They made moving patterns on the rough linen.

Someone or something was writing to her again. Another message? Everywhere she turned, she found pictographs, ideograms, alphabets, hieroglyphs. Things were writing to her, using the shadows of matter like a holy debris from the light, writing against the hours flying.

Laughter came through the window—who, or what, was laughing? Claire went upstairs into a bedroom. *You can't get away*, the voice said. She realized she must get away from the apartment. After supper, she thought, and then she realized she could not eat the chicken that John was cooking.

Poulet, that was the word—the poulet had been caught and killed. Claire saw John and Aunt Ella Vator with axes and knives. The voice confirmed it, *Yes, they are your enemies; they are bloodthirsty murderers. They will murder you,* the voice hissed. No, Claire thought, no. The voices spoke to one another: *She has no say about it, she is the poor lay, poor lamb, lambasted.* Claire put on a sweater and tip-toed down the stairs.

She took a little winding side street through the village. The swifts darted down into the street and led the way to the mountains. As she climbed the steep path on the other side of the river, the voices were quiet. She looked down on a green paradise above the rushing water. The town below was receding, the houses the size of houses in a Monopoly game.

The path twisted and turned, taking her up. In the far distance, she saw the limestone face of a peak lit by the sun, and suddenly, an old man with a beard standing on the path. "Bonjour Madame," he began and continued to speak in a rippling stream of French, whose sounds echoed without meaning.

The sun was setting when the shale slipped under her feet. Her heartbeat rose. The green of the woods was beneath her now and the color of the world receded into the sky. Claire spotted a wooden staff by the side of the path, picked it up, and tested it for solidity. It had a natural handle; perhaps it had been left there for her. It certainly made her climb a little easier. Her throat was dry and she wished she'd brought her water bottle.

The voices were still silent. She was grateful for that and yet unsure of what to do without them. She thought of John and Aunt Ella Vator. She held the image of her aunt's smile and felt the wonder of John's steady presence over the past ten years. Could they be murderers? Were the voices misleading her? But without the voices, she could do nothing; she would be nothing.

Claire continued her climb toward the peak.

When the voices returned, they were not at all clear. They whispered and shouted syllables, and just as something was connecting, it disconnected: *tugabug serves too many tags galaxy morning tea ma magical arc.* Sentence fragments floated on a wave of syntax without sense: *the tease is up, tracking the future in light, two continents colliding, it won't be in books, heraldic leaf spears.*

With these fragments images came without sense or order, first the cut-out line of the trees and the horizon, all distances shortened in the growing dusk, and closer to her, as if guiding her up the path, the shapes of letters appearing, disappearing, the ascending slope of the *A*, the open bowl of *C*, the waiting drop of a lowercase *r*.

These letters twinkled in and out of existence, her passport into another time, as the sounds of the woods and the voices made a cacophony around her.

Claire sat to think. What if the voices were misleading? What if she did not follow them? She held her head with her hands over her ears but it made no difference. She tried to decipher the letters she had seen: *A* is the saving letter, the indefinite article, 'at' in a circle, toward the city, ace, and upside down, 'given any.'

R the canine letter, the growl, Latin for take, as in a recipe, take a pinch of salt, a bit of poison, this or that, *R* for the set of real numbers, *r* for the radius of a circle; *C* as one hundred, *CM* nine hundred—had she subtracted and added the numbers correctly earlier in the day? *C* as caput, the head beheaded; *c* for currere, to run; *c* in $E = mc$ squared; square, triangle, circle, cup, cross current, a seal, a lock to open, what is to come?

And then Claire saw it in the darkness: a light veil extending down to the edge of the path, a net like lace, but made of light. On the other side, a voice called out her name. She lifted the veil and stepped under it.

Clear as a Bell

And I could hear no sound/ as far as I could hear except a round kind of echo without end.

—Patricia Kathleen Page

Tommy watched the light scatter on the wood floor. A fleeting sail of brightness crossed the edge of the carpet when the outer gate opened to its apex to admit the next patient. He had begun seeing his patients in person at his home office once more by June 2022, at least the younger ones. Many patients still attended their sessions via Zoom. But whether he had been absorbed in listening in person or remotely, his closing words were always the same, "We'll leave it there for today."

It was a fine summer morning. He turned the air conditioner on and then off again. He did not like the smell of metal nor the cold air and moved away to the tall window and opened it with a little jerk of his wrists. Ventilation was better. The morning air on his face was warm already and it reminded him of something he could not name.

He saw a flurry of small hands and remembered a game of 'topping hands,' and he thought that the pleasure was not in the slaps, which stung his hands, nor in the delivery of his own slaps, but in the blurred moments between slaps when he did not know whether his hands could be extricated from the pile and hit the top again.

This, he thought, was more like the listening he did when he was most present, when words came like a torrent and he heard their sounds from elsewhere, from a gap that opened between what was said and what was not yet known.

He shut the window. He stood on his toes and stretched his arms above his head, reaching up until his fingers grazed the edge of the casement. He cracked his knuckles lightly and ran his right hand down along the polished cotton of his white shirt. He repeated the gesture, his fingers gliding over the little rounds of buttons on the mound of his torso.

He went tie-less with his old analysands, but always put on a tie to meet a new patient. Now he lifted the yellow one with blue fleurs-de-lis from the bottom drawer of his desk and closed his eyes to feel the motions of the ritual more keenly. His hands flew through the dance with the tie. He held one end and lifted the knot, pulling it taut.

This was the interval when he usually looked over his notes from the previous session, not so much to renew his memory as to revisit his questions. But with a new patient, there were no notes to review. He took out a fresh legal pad, checked his pen cartridge, and sat fiddling with the black Lamy. His mind empty suddenly, he broke into a sweat. A new patient always induced this reaction in him, and yet it surprised him each time.

This first meeting would likely reveal something the patient would do anything to avoid, something that had already happened and yet was happening again—to the patient's consternation. The thing each patient turned away from was Tommy's ally in the work. It took a long time, of course, to winnow away long held illusions and come to see it clearly. Each time, Tommy knew the work would require courage, and he didn't presume to know if he *had* the store of courage that would be required.

Her name was Eloise Rainer, and Tommy was struck by her youth. She sat very still in her chair in her pink mask. He did not invite her to lie on his couch, wanting to hear her reason for seeking him out first. Long brown hair tucked behind her ears, she looked down and said nothing. After ten minutes or so, he saw that she was crying. Tears in a first session were not unusual but a prolonged silence was.

After twenty minutes, Tommy settled in with it, and his mind flew into its own spaces. He could sit for hours, days, in this threaded time of waiting. If he didn't sit in silence so much of the time, he might not have such a space within himself for the intangible, unfinished, and repeating thoughts that came to him now.

He thought of the patience of trees stripped in a rain in November. How they have some bleak alternative to dying, some way of waiting under wind, snow, and ice. He thought of Ben searching the hillside for his brother when they were sledding. He thought about the dead and still dying in his own city, the long lockdown and silence and the birds singing in it, the banging of pots each evening, the refrigerator trucks full of bodies.

Where was his daughter now? Was she alive and well? Catherine had been wearing a red coat when he last saw her. He thought of the tricycle in the hallway when he came home from the airport without her, its little bell on the handlebar. As she rode up and down the hall, he'd sat at the foot of the stairs handing out or collecting 'tickets' from a stack of paper scraps.

The diminishing sound of that bell imploded in him. These sounds and images came to him.

The young woman before him did not lift her face, nor reach for a Kleenex. Her mask was soaked with tears and snot. Whatever it was she was crying about seemed to take her entirely outside of words, even gestures.

She would speak when it was possible. For now, he could only wait.

Tommy entered the kitchen by a detour into the front hallway to retrieve the day's mail on the library table. He put the bills to one side and riffled through the *Restoration Hardware* catalog until he came to the cups and saucers and remembered his espresso. Julie made it for him before she went off to her teach her art class each morning in Red Hook, timing it for his 11am break. He sipped from the tiny cup and closed his eyes to savor it.

But only for a moment because Freud jumped up on the table and walked under his arm, jostling the cup ever so lightly with his tail. He wondered if Ms. Rainer would return. Sometimes a young person would put an end to the whole analytic enterprise before it had ever begun. He pictured her head bent looking at the floor, how she'd turned to look at the window and the dilation of her pupils when she finally looked at him.

He'd seen her fear, and then something else designed to cover it. What stayed with him though was the fear he'd seen. Absently, his hand slid over Freud's smooth back and the cat arched under his hand for a second before hopping down. He swallowed the last of the warm liquid and rinsed his cup.

His next patient was the son of a New York mobster who still met Tommy on Zoom. Jim Baretti, now in his fifties, had left his family to protect his adolescent children

132

from inevitably becoming part of the family business. But he did not feel part of the new world he'd joined by forsaking his place in the mob, changing even his given name.

Tommy heard about gambling, murder, and money (and oh that great plumb line of the dream into guilt) in Mr. Baretti's sessions. It was likely that the original reason for guilt lay beyond what Mr. Baretti could say, even now.

His patient, lying on a couch in his own living room, had placed his laptop on a table behind him so that Tommy was positioned just where he would sit in the office. Mr. Baretti stretched out, yawned, and began with a dream:

"We get on the bus to go back home, carrying many bags. I'm on the platform at Avenue *U*. A newspaper slips from my father's hand to the ground. An obituary page falls open. The name is 'Upendsky.' There is someone who looks like a man but it's a woman leaning over a table, working with fine tools of some kind."

Tommy waited to see what his patient would do with the dream. Mr. Baretti shifted on the couch, cleared his throat. "My mother had a big black pocketbook, the kind with a gold clasp, and she crammed it full of stuff. I carried the shopping bags for her, but I was always intrigued by her pocketbook, and I never got to carry that. She was always afraid my father was going to get popped off." His patient stopped there.

"Popped off?" Tommy wondered.

Mr. Baretti laughed. "I mean killed. My grandfather was Pops. Pops could kill my dad. I knew that was possible. I knew my mother was afraid of that. I wasn't though. I thought my dad was invincible. And he was fun. He used to

133

read the newspaper just to laugh at the world and the way it worked."

Tommy said nothing.

"When I was a boy, I walked to school by a basement watch shop, and looked down to see a man working, bent over some intricate work. I wanted to mend watches when I grew up, and knew it wasn't what my father had in mind for me."

"Upendsky?" Tommy inquired, intrigued by the unusual name.

"There was a view down and a view up from the basement shop where the man worked. He did not ever look up to see me. I looked down on him. My father looked down on everyone. But the word is up. Up end. Once, when I was about five, my father took me to a park; there was a bench and he climbed up on it, and I went up, too. Then he lifted me, upended me, and held me dangling upside down." It felt like a long time. Mr. Baretti paused. "Did he do that? Why would he do that?"

Tommy knew it was not possible for his patient to verify what may have indeed happened, or what may have been a fantasy. This distinction didn't matter now anyway: they were in another scene, another logic.

"There's a bench in your dream. The person at the bench looks like a man but is a woman?" Tommy asks.

"Yeah. Why is it a woman? The name is from an obituary, so someone's dead. The man in the watch shop, yeah looked like a woman in the dream. I wanted to be him."

He hesitated. "I wanted to be *her*?" Mr. Baretti was completely baffled.

"We'll stop there today," Tommy said.

He sat looking over his notes. He ended the session there so that his patient would not close off his question with some all too eager explanation and would dream again. It almost always worked. Mr. Baretti had been in analysis now for five years and knew very well that his dreams held the answers he needed, and his analyst did not have any of the answers, after all.

But his patients' dreams sometimes left a residue in Tommy, and though it no longer surprised him, sometimes he felt as though a patient's dream could have easily been his. This dream was such a dream.

Tommy walked out into the fine June day to join Max at the local luncheonette. It had seating on the front sidewalk, but maybe they could risk eating inside. It was hot out. They'd met long ago, when Tommy was learning to treat children and Max was the supervising analyst. Speaking of children's play, Max had said once, "God's in the details," and that comment stayed with Tommy.

Max was late but Tommy knew he'd be a little late, not too much, just a little, as if to remind them that it was possible to be a bit late in their scheduled lives, and not have it matter so very much. Max was the funniest analyst Tommy knew; without half trying, he made the world a bright and quirky place.

Tommy took a booth by the door near an open window and fan (safe enough) where he could observe the street. So many old people going by, walking step by careful step. Would he walk like that someday? Here is a fat woman in a white mask, her feet angled out, so as not to trip, and another skinny one with a brown cane, her face in sunglasses craning up like a turtle's head.

Here comes Max himself in his over-sized brown linen jacket, in his pink and green striped shirt, hands locked behind him. Strolling along, looking around, stepping over the threshold now, he walks as if in a dream. Max takes off his slightly bashed straw hat and uncovers a white curly head. Here are the lines that come between his dark eyebrows, furrowed in thought.

"Everything I say I regret saying. What if I just didn't speak, Tommy?" he said, by way of a greeting.

"Then I'd order you one of those garden vegan salads and you'd be unhappy."

Max nodded. "That would not do. All morning I've been thinking of a cheeseburger deluxe, rippled potato chips on the side."

"What did you say, by the way?"

"I said, 'Get rid of the poisonous snake the kid keeps letting out of the cage.' They got him a Rottweiler instead." Max could not say more about the case and Tommy didn't ask.

Max created spaces to think in a conversation, and so they ate their respective cheeseburger deluxe and roast beef with horseradish on rye in an amiable silence.

Tommy looked over at two young women laughing uproariously at the counter. One wore six braids in her lank blond hair; the other had a streak of red dyed into her black head, all the hair piled up with a string, like a package.

Would Catherine look like that? Would she prefer the vegan menu? Was there anything deluxe on it? Were there limits to deluxe? Would she have liked his favorite treat—

peaches covered in honey and nuts? Would she have read his old *Tin Tin* comics? Would she have wanted a beagle, a baby turtle, or a snake as a pet? Would she go with him to Coney Island now if she were here?

Max wiped his mouth. "You were eyeing that piece of cake to have with your coffee. What does your heart need with seven-layer Mocha Crème Cake? Forget it, forget it. Have a slice of watermelon." And he saw Tommy's face drop.

"I know what we can do. Let's spend the day on the subway. I know it's hot out there but it's not too hot. The analysands can have the afternoon off."

Tommy laughed. "Yeah. Let's go to Coney Island. We can take the F train there and be back by 5pm." They sipped their coffee.

"How's Freud?" Max asked as he set down the tip.

"Oh, I can't answer that. I think he's had an affair with Minna, the cat next door, not the sister-in-law."

Max roared at that and Tommy felt better; yes much better.

Tommy had two more Zoom patients before his last in-person appointment of the day. Michael was a young man who had come to Tommy after a second hospitalization when he was just twenty years old. Tommy was not sure he could do anything to make any difference. For the first year or so, his patient was evidently terrified almost all the time, and yet there was no sign of transference to his analyst.

Instinctively, Tommy didn't invite him to lie on the couch. Michael wore sunglasses to his sessions and kept his face averted. This was not because he was doing serious drugs or felt he had something to hide. Far from struggling to hide secrets he didn't want Tommy to know, Michael felt he had no place and no right to hide anything at all.

He wore sunglasses to protect against his conviction that Tommy could see into his mind and scramble his thoughts if he had access to his eyes. Michael had turned his head away so that he could see Tommy's gestures, since gestures cannot lie. But then, three years into his analysis, Michael came to his session without the sunglasses one day, and though he was frozen in his fright, he never retreated to wearing the glasses again.

He spoke more easily most of the time now. In fact, he was eloquent once he realized that Tommy had no intention of seeing into his mind, or telling him what was real, or interrupting him to interpret his experiences.

Michael sat in his chair in a rumpled, clean white shirt and blue jeans, looking younger than twenty-three. Michael had recently begun to write poetry. He brought Tommy his poems, the finished ones, not the ones that were still in the making. He told Tommy, "They're not for analysis," and that was that.

He sometimes read to Tommy, and at such times, his analyst felt himself in the presence of hearing things he'd never been able to say, glittering moments of recognition.

Tommy was the single person Michael spoke to when he wasn't quite sure he should do. In his dream, he told Tommy, "A woman said, 'Get people on a boat to the North.' The next day, I saw in the *New York Times* that the virus was rising in the South." Michael paused. "I didn't say it to anyone—that they should go north over the water. I didn't get through to anyone, and some of them died. I've thought of a plan, though."

"What is your plan?" Tommy asked.

"Even now, three should go ahead. A kind of trinity."

"Which three should go?" Tommy asked.

"I was waiting for the next dream to tell me that."

Tommy said, "I don't think it was your fault. I don't think you could have done anything for those people." Michael seemed relieved, at least in that moment. Tommy ended the session on that note.

Back in the kitchen, Tommy made himself a glass of iced tea. He shook out a little packet of Splenda and tore off one corner, leaving the blue letters against the yellow envelope intact. In the last wash, Julie uncovered a pocket filled with these little yellow packets. Yes, he told her, he had a habit of carrying a small supply around.

Splenda was splendid for his weight. There were Kleenexes his wife didn't find, too. They had dried to new shapes: pocket sculptures—they shredded as he fished them out. Everything was in a process of disintegration, falling apart. Splenda had an 'end' in it, too. He remembered 'up end sky' and saw a sky with revolving clouds in a river below.

He stirred the Splenda into his cup, pushing the spoon back and forth, not around in a circle. His mind moved like this: toward and in retreat, for and against, a storm in a teacup—over nothing, what tie to wear! The result was indecision, impasse.

He needed a bit of Splenda for his tomato base and reached into his pocket for another packet. He turned from the saucepan to his chopping board and the shallots waiting in a bowl and thought of Nora's jingle. What was it? 'In flew end za,' influenza. That was about the last pandemic, the Spanish flu of 1918. It was also prescient.

"God is in the details," Max often said, his signature for things other people just didn't notice. But what details, Tommy wondered, when you couldn't possibly keep track of them all? Distracting details were shaping his life, and probably his death—but how? He'd stirred a cup of coffee at an airport counter twenty years ago and his child had been carried away without his noticing—until it was too late.

He couldn't act. Mr. Baretti could act, could account for his acts. He could protect his own children. Michael could act, too; moving against his own strange ideas, he'd speak to Tommy.

Julie came in the door to find Tommy wiping his eyes over a pile of finely chopped shallots. She walked across the tiles and stood behind him, rested her cheek against his broad back, and said, "Were you weeping for the Lady of Shallot?"

Tommy recited, "'There she weaves by night and day...' how did it go?"

"What were you thinking about?" Julie asked.

"Distracting details," he sighed.

"Oh, yes. Now I remember another line: 'A curse is on her if she stay.'"

He turned. "Is there a curse on you?" he asked, lifting her chin to see her face.

She smiled at him. "I don't know. Do you believe in curses?" She looked over at the cat curled under the small lamp on the counter where Tommy had opened a bottle of merlot. "Freud believes in curses, doesn't he?"

"He believes we're thrust into catastrophe by things we don't want to know. You could think of it as a curse," Tommy mused.

He set out the prime rib with tomato shallot sauce, surrounded by blanched green beans right from the garden.

"You're stacking things now—I'll never want to eat out again," Julie commented.

"It's safer for us to eat at home anyway. I saw a pyramid of 'Tokal' beans in Asher's window. The cans were stacked in a pyramid. It wasn't the pyramid that did it; it was the shapes of the beans against the blue labels."

"Not unlike Monet's haystacks?" she teased.

He looked down at the plates in the slanted evening sun. "Not unlike," he agreed. As they settled into eating, there was not much Tommy could say about his day, except for his lunch with Max. He told Julie about the way old people walk, step by careful step, and how Max was never in any hurry, or at least he gave that impression.

Julie was beautiful, he thought, even more so at fifty-two with her high cheekbones and face sculpted to carry an experience of the world missing in her youth. However, her suffering didn't show in her face. She had a natural ebullience. Was she still in love with him? Maybe not the original Tommy, but she loved him—his quirks, failings, the odd ways his mind moved. And yes, she loved his body, the expanse of him so foreign to her.

She was asking him something. "Will we stay put and work on the weeds, or meet Peter and Helen at the park?"

"I can happily pull weeds and not listen to Helen going on about her newest antiques, and I've made peach sorbet for later. Can we get by without going?"

Tommy poured second glasses of wine and carried them to the screened-in porch. Julie came downstairs in work pants and a rumpled blue shirt, a pile of old newspapers tucked under her arm. She set them down on the table. At once, Freud jumped up to spread his full length on them, his tabby gray stripes widening from his soft white belly.

Julie eased out a sheet from under the cat and the pile, cut it to ribbons, and dunked them in a shallow rubber basin. She lifted them, dripping, into a big sieve over a galvanized bucket. She would mix wet paper and straw to mulch in the cool of the evening, after the weeds were finished.

Tommy loved the screened-in porch, an addition to their Brooklyn brownstone that cost them not too much of the backyard. It had a white wooden frame, with screens on three sides and a tilting roof, an outdoor room of sorts. This room, even before it was built, most resembled the rooms of his childhood summers on Cape Cod.

There he could smell the ocean, hear the voices of his grandparents, see the puzzle pieces inside the finished frame on the old card table. As a child, he'd mailed home rocks, dune grasses, shells, once the carapace of a hermit crab, as if he could reassemble this world and all its echoes back in St. Louis.

Tommy moved up and down the raised beds, plucking weeds between rows of carrots, beans, potatoes, and new beet tops. In early June, the asparagus was ready for picking beneath impossibly fine sprays of green. When he'd made these beds two years ago, at the start of the pandemic, he built in benches along the sides for comfort in weeding. He always used them. Julie did not, but then she was younger.

He opened the water spigot to drip irrigate the beds and run the sprinkler at the same time. Narrow and sunlit, two feet high, his beds fed them well. Julie was finishing with the straw and wet newspapers where he'd weeded. Tommy crossed the lawn after calculating the arc of the sprinkler.

He stood in the doorway. The eye of the day was closing, and beyond the darkening porch, he saw the light in the kitchen. His daughter could enter now from that backlight, looking very much like Eloise Rainer. He turned the lamps on in the porch and went into the kitchen to retrieve the peach sorbet from the freezer. He was lost in currents of what could never be and missing what was right here before him.

Julie came into the kitchen with a handful of yellow roses and he saw her jiggle them into an arrangement that seemed to assemble itself in the small vase. He could not cipher why her hands shot him through with a longing that reached his stomach and his groin; he could not attend to it all. He put two spoons by the little dessert bowls.

He loved the spoons for what they were, and the peach sorbet for what he'd made, and his wife for staying with him in the ruins of what had happened.

Freud kicked Julie's gardening gloves aside with his hind feet and took up his place next to the lamp. They laughed and lifted their spoons.

Tommy was propped against two pillows, a light blanket over his lap, with Lacan's Seminar on *The Formations of the Unconscious*. Julie was immersed in Maupassant's *Pierre et Jean*. She threw off the covers suddenly in one of her 'power surges' or night sweats. Tommy had given her a series of artsy paper fans, and she brandished one now, stirring the air with vigor as her eyes followed the print.

Tommy was usually ready with a 'listen to this' from Lacan, but he'd learned to contain his impulse to read aloud and puzzle the enigma of his reading when Julie was intent on her own reading. Freud blinked, turned twice, started his rumbling purr, and slept on the end of the bed.

Tommy woke up in the dim room and went to the bathroom to relieve himself. He had the vestige of a dream in his mind. He closed the toilet lid, turned on the light, and reached for the small book, his dream journal, beside his reading glasses and the pen he kept on the window ledge. He could not recall everything, so he wrote from the dream fragments he retained:

A dog is tethered to a post, but his collar is not latched. He strolls off. A courteous child protests, but no one pays her any mind.

While still sleepy, Tommy wrote out his first associations, a habit after over a decade in his own analysis. A dog reminded him of the shape of a dog from behind, outlined against a window, gazing at something. Stroll—he thought of Max's walk, an amble. Strolled off reminded his of Mr. Baretti's 'popped off'—the anxiety of death.

He saw the dog's collar unlatched, its buckle open, a limp strap hanging. Buckle down could mean attend. He imagined a seat harness for a child, without the child. Tommy gasped as stroll became 'stroller' and he saw it empty. A courteous child protests. Catherine was just learning to say 'please and thank you,' but she was more

144

than likely to put up a storm of protest, especially when her exploring was curtailed.

She was learning not to kick and scream when she was angry. "No kicking," he would say, and she would stop. He remembered her protesting the stroller though, a work of stiffened legs and a twisting wrench away.

He realized for the first time, he'd never put her into that stroller—she would have had a tantrum and he'd wanted to avoid that embarrassment at the airport. She must have wandered off from where she was playing by the suitcases. If a stranger had picked her up near him, she'd have called out to him. He'd thought of her as tethered to him through his gaze—confident that she never went out of his sight. But the tether had broken that day.

The intersection of the words of his dream and associations made a new version of memory that drove him out to the screened-in porch. Freud padded behind him. The world wobbled now, tilted on a new axis. Was he more at fault, or less, for never having strapped her into the stroller? He opened the back door and stepped out on the cool steps in his bare feet.

It was a clear night, a night with a suggestion of stars, even in Brooklyn. He thought of Ben, Sarah, Nora, and Claire—what a different story he would have to tell them now. But would he? What words would suffice to say any of this?

He lifted Freud, and the cat stretched out all along his forearm. He remembered lifting his daughter as a baby, the acrid smell of wet diaper, the sweetness of her neck. He wanted her in her crib again now, before the age of protest and courtesy, the clock going forward, the night air coming in from an open window. He would hold her in his arms and she would be safe.

With a sinking heart, he sat down on the cool step, still holding the cat. It was clear as a bell that he hadn't put her into the stroller.

Après Coup

It is when you are asking about something that you realize you yourself have survived it, and so you must carry it, or fashion it into a thing that carries itself.

—Anne Carson

What was he doing at a train station in Montreal? All during the pandemic, Ben thought of his friends and considered taking a train journey again, as people for centuries took a pilgrimage after an illness. Ben suffered through a tough case of Covid-19 but he survived when so many had not. Mostly exhausted for three weeks with weighted limbs, a whole body fatigue, he wondered if he'd ever be the same, if this was the dreaded 'long Covid'?

But it wasn't. By the time it was possible to travel on a train again, nearly three years had passed since he and his friends had been together. Would they do it again? Even supposing? No matter the consequences? Toward what end? Ben asked himself over and over. He didn't know, so he muttered indignant phrases while he considered it, rejecting each impulse to go ahead and email the others. But, in the end, he knew that they would come back together.

It was October 2022 when they boarded a train once more, this time from Montreal to Halifax, in Nova Scotia, a Canadian coastal route that would begin in the evening with one overnight, arriving in the evening of the following day. They could overnight in Canada and return independently.

Ben joined the line of passengers and climbed up onto the train, the 'Océan.' Ahead of him, he saw Tommy navigating a narrow, sleek corridor and followed him to their sleeping car, more spacious than Amtrak's, with their own private bathroom. An announcement came in French and in English that the dining car was opening now for dinner.

They hurried to join the women. Everyone seemed pleased with Ben's choice of train and this Canadian adventure.

"Where is Claire?" Sarah asked, suddenly aware that they were four, not five. "Is she late? Was she not able to make it this time?"

Ben looked at his friends and spoke only the bare facts: "No, Claire will not make it. In response to my email invitation, John called me to say that she did not live through the pandemic. She had a mental crisis of some kind in the Pyrenees. He took her to a rural hospital, she contracted Covid there and did not make it out again. There was no funeral." He hesitated, "It was just not possible."

Ben looked at his friends. They were stunned and he could not reverse his words. What had been the bad news that he carried up until this moment was now beyond him.

Tommy noticed a small wooden boat painted red, sitting near the windowsill, behind the flowers on their pristine white tablecloth. Left behind by a child?

Sarah said, "I knew it would happen to someone I knew but not to Claire."

Nora asked, "When did you find out?"

Ben sighed. "A few weeks ago. I did not want to tell you in an email or on the phone. I wanted us to be here together again."

Sarah spoke sharply, "We are not together again; everything has changed."

They sat in silence. They were crossing a river. St. Lawrence? Ben wondered. His friends remained quiet for a long time. A waiter came by with a wine card and dinner menus. Tommy reached for them and gestured the man away. Nora felt tears bloom in her eyes. She put her glasses on her nose, ostensibly to read the dinner menu, but mostly to soften and hide her sudden sorrow.

Yes, they'd have wine. "What's it to be?" Tommy asked.

Ben said, "19 Crimes." He was partial to the brand, notable for taste as well as its corks, one for each of the nineteen crimes a person could commit to be sentenced to 'Punishment by Transportation to Australia,' for life. Ben asked the waiter for the cork. Each had the name of the crime on the side. Tonight's was 'Petty larceny. Theft under one shilling.'

Sarah quipped, "We're all criminals." With that, they all laughed, even Nora.

And the dinner was wonderful, not only the fresh salmon, crisp green beans, and chocolate cake, but also their long comfortable silences, broken by the soft clinking of forks and knives, a time for taking in the sad news when they could be lost in their own thoughts.

Claire remained a presence all through and after dinner, not so much a ghost now as the hologram of the last time they were together, as she pulled out the cards, showing them the Mirdek card cipher system. They moved to the women's private suite on the upper deck. It was spacious with a table that folded down between two sofas that would later convert to beds.

As if on cue, Ben drew out the deck of playing cards from his backpack.

"John sent them to me. It's Claire's word game; he thought she would want us to continue. Let's do this again."

"Okay. I will try to do this again. Did anyone bring the Mirdek?" Tommy began. Ben slid it across the table to him. Seeing they had no coin, Tommy took a penny from his pocket, selected a card, and counted letters under the red second half of the alphabet, arriving at *S*.

"You can begin to lose your sense of position while looking at the sky. You know that feeling of falling upward? 'The eye loses itself in the depths, having no limit or resting place.' That's from a man who wrote about the sky in 1282.

"I wrote that line down on a napkin in Barcelona when I went searching for my daughter this past spring. My Catherine would be twenty-five now. I thought she may have been taken out of the country as a child, so I put my finger on a spinning globe and when it stopped, there was Barcelona under my index finger.

"Then, now; time pleated up like an accordion. I didn't find my daughter, but at least I went searching. I can't be certain she survived this pandemic. Young people, contrary to popular opinion, did die.

"There's a lifetime of things that happened in the last few years. Julie left me just after I lost our child. But she returned to me and she stayed. She has come to love me with my flaws, even the flaws that have cost her too much. And through her eyes, I can forgive myself. At moments, anyway.

"Mostly I remember ordinary pandemic moments: a child's discarded Mickey-Mouse themed mask on a sidewalk, running out of paper clips for my patient files, eating pancakes on a weekday morning with sunlight flooding the table. Worry, too, like an unwanted guest that went everywhere with you."

Tommy hesitated.

"I can't get over the idea that Claire isn't here. It wasn't her first breakdown, you know. She's had these episodes since our college years at least. And she made sketchbooks. There must be many of these and I wonder where they are."

He shook his head, stood up, and stretched. "I'll go get us cookies."

It was growing dark when Tommy returned. He put his copper penny on the table next to the cookies.

Ben noticed that the sound of the train changed as they moved over a bridge, as though the air underneath made an echo chamber. He picked up the penny. It was a bit bigger than the original centime.

"Something I have not been able to say: Even before the news about Claire, even before we began the word game. Nora and Claire and I all lost a family member when we were children. That loss has shadowed my whole life. I see Martin's canaries perched on a swing in their cage, out in our sun porch. Their little feet are the color of eggplant.

"I see sun on snow, yellow and periwinkle shadows. We are sledding, sleds and saucers and tires flying by and everyone screaming. He is out there without me, his red jacket vanishing. He is everywhere on that snowy hillside, running and yelling. I'm in charge of him but I can't find him. It is dark and I'm stumbling, falling. I'm cold but I can't go home without him.

"I'm falling as if he's already dead, as if it's already my fault, as if I know that I will have to replace him and can never take his place. He is gone and everywhere; I can't find him, nor speak to him.

"Now Claire, like Martin, is vast space. She's the invisible dimension of something approaching and disappearing. Time becomes a loop in this kind of company."

He was quiet and his friends waited.

He put the penny down.

Nora looked out and only saw her reflection in the train window. She picked up the coin.

"During the time of the pandemic I was in Dublin, working on a project about infinity with a wonderful young man, Cían, a poet from Kerry. Time is stranger than you might suppose, and Claire's presence among us more complicated than we might imagine.

"Just say we go through a little thought experiment. In the early 1900s, Einstein elevated light to the true constant of the universe. Time was not absolute; light was. Time and space were connected through a shaft of pure light. This changed everything.

"Music was no longer the thing it had been for centuries, a thing made up of oscillating molecules. It glowed incandescent. Music could be converted into light. In fact, it had happened *already*. In 1886, Heinrich Hertz discovered an electromagnetic wave—with a very, very long wavelength. The wavelength of visible light, the distance between peaks, is measured in nanometers.

"A nanometer is one of twenty-five million, four hundred thousand parts of an inch! The distance in Hertz's waves could be measured out in feet between peaks, even in miles. These waves were a form of radiant energy. Hertz called them 'radio waves.' Reporters asked him what use they might have and Hertz didn't know of any use whatsoever.

"In 1895, less than ten years later, Guglielmo Marconi converted agitated molecules of sound into light, in the form of radio waves. He built antenna in the shape of Gothic spires, towers reaching into the sky. And though the spires at Chartres were mute, Marconi's towers vibrated with light that was music.

"This form of light could travel out in all directions at one hundred eighty-six thousand miles per second. Space contracted. A vast electromagnetic net was cast over all of humankind. Wherever we go in our time, we are immersed in this gossamer veil we can't see.

"And here's something else to consider. The ionosphere reflects those radio waves back to the earth, where they pick up even more light. Then they bounce off and move out beyond the curvature of the globe. Bach and Mozart, Phillip Glass, recent music I know nothing about, and all the news on the radio in every language, all this resounds in space, traveling on light waves from our tiny planet.

"But light is also moving toward us. Light has been moving toward us since the beginning of time. *What* is unfolding in each of us and making a future already written in light? Even what we are saying now, even Claire's voice three years ago, was that a future that was there already, there from the very beginning?"

Nora let her question hang in the air. She put the coin down near Sarah.

Sarah shook her head and smiled. She'd been impatient with Nora's historic exposition, but that agitation had suddenly vanished.

"Nora, what you say makes me dizzy. Last summer, I was looking at the stars with my granddaughter, Tyler, on a particularly clear night in the Ozarks, during a family vacation. She was fifteen at the time. I can name the constellations from memory, from my summer camp days: 'Big and little dippers; the seven sisters, Orion's belt.' 'Where's the rest of him?' Tyler asks. I have no answer.

"She says: 'There's the Moose's House.' 'Whose house?' I ask, incredulous, 'Where did you learn that?' She rolls her eyes. 'Yeah, and look, over there's the Fox-boy, see his long snout raised in a howl?' She laughs. 'And there,' I join in, 'see the Lighthouse, winking?' 'That's Venus,' she says with authority, reversing things.

"We have built a fire and it is growing dim. We bundle up in extra clothes for pillows, lie down and settle. In the silence, you can hear the wind in the pines and the fire crackling nearby, sending up sparks. While the stars blink down at us, I wonder what Tyler will remember of this time of pandemic when she was a teenager.

"I think of all the intangible things you cannot give anyone. So much of our lives is lost, but then so much is invented on the spot, out of nowhere."

She put the coin down and they sat together and polished off the cookies.

Nora was curious to see the observation car at one end of the upper deck of the train. Sarah followed her, and sure enough, the stars were visible through the curved ceiling of glass.

Tommy woke when the train stopped around the middle of the night at a station in Sainte Foy, where many departed the train to take a shuttle into Quebec City. He felt a pang of longing to return to that beautiful old city where he'd done much of his psychoanalytic training. He could picture the streets with their beautiful old buildings, the hilly city geography with its stairs, the city park by the St. Lawrence River, and its exquisite little art museum.

He could smell the croissants in his favorite bakery. Not this time, he reminded himself, as he listened to the passengers leaving.

Sarah woke early, restless in her berth. She pushed the blind up and let in a crack of strong light, blinked, adjusted her eyes, and pushed it up more. The train was going over a

157

river, she did not know where. She glimpsed a fly fisherman out in the middle, his line looping in a beautiful long *S*. "Wake up," she said aloud to Nora, who turned over and groaned.

"It's our only day. So much to say!" Sarah chided. Then she put on her robe and went to wake Ben and Tommy in their car downstairs.

At 7:48am they entered the town of Compelton. Ben, checking his watch and his timetable, was astonished that the train was exactly on time. The sky was clear blue, yet early in October they could see Sugar Loaf Mountain with snow on top. Tommy quipped, "My French toast is also dusted with something like snow," as he took a first, satisfyingly sweet bite.

"We don't have all day," Sarah said as she urged her friends to leave for the upper deck and get to the game.

Ben said, "We do have all day! Let's top up our coffees first." And coffees in hand, they settled in their private car on the upper deck.

Nora picked up the penny, selected the card, and was stumped by it. A Jack with no face? A Joker? The letter *K* did not inspire her.

Her mind flew through some *K* possibilities. Kelvin temperature scale. Kepler's Laws. Kilogram. Kilowatt Hour. Kinematics. Kinetic Energy. None of them suited her.

She wondered about substituting another letter; after all, who would know?

Her commitment to stay in the constraints of the game won out, however.

"Give me a minute," she said.

"As a child, I imagined that my father was looking at me, even when he wasn't there, as if my father's blind eyes were all-seeing. And I could almost hear him thinking about me. I can't tell you what that kindled in me!

"Sometimes I have that feeling about my iPhone now, that it is keeping track of me; I mean it has the same effect. My father, long dead, looks at me from that tiny screen."

She put the coin down.

Tommy picked it up and decided to go with Nora's last word.

"When I think of a screen, I think of Freud. My cat's name is Freud. Go ahead, laugh—an analyst with a cat named Freud. Most people think a cat is very self-contained, and in a way, this is true. If Freud can't be bothered, he looks bored, and then he rolls over and sleeps.

"But it's interesting to me that every time something new emerges with a patient, Freud will hop up under my hand, walk directly under my hand, as if to mark that something has happened for me by jostling my palm. He wasn't there with the patient; only I was, but when he does this, I know I have carried something from a session into the room with him. Freud knows what I don't yet recognize. Strange, isn't it?"

He put the coin back.

Sarah held her warm cup in one hand, the penny in the other, and wondered what to say.

"Everywhere you look now, people are looking at screens. Kindles, iPads, iPhones; we take them everywhere and live our lives through them. Tyler went to school on screens for more than a year and came to hate them. But now, she's back with her screens, almost all the time. But for me the book, the paper book with pages—that's the real thing.

"I want to devour pages, one by one, and then go back to the start. I remember reading to my children when they were just forming their first words. They seemed to understand what I was reading. Those books did not seem to frighten them, not even the scary ones, the grim ones. They would ask me to read them over and over. But who knows what children feel and cannot say?"

She put the coin down. They waited.

Ben had no idea what the word was, or even the letter, yet he picked up the coin.

"If I could speak as the child I was, if I could, what would I want to say?" He stopped, looked out on an expanse of water. Still a river, or lake, or a flood plain?

"I'd say what I couldn't then: Open the box, take out from between the creases of tissue paper, the new shoes you do not deserve. Remember licorice whips stolen opening out into lengths of clothesline, a belt stinging fear into the body, all its strands distinct.

"Refold this tale, in the cloakroom, licorice in your pocket, with the sour smell of winter coats and boots. Brimful, the milk spills, a shadow on the white cloth, damp, and souring. Brimful of tension, you carry your cup with stiff steps attentive to every tilt and swaying up to the edge; a wave as you surf your cup of cocoa to the table and slurp, burning the soft inside of your lips, a sharp pain that turns dim, as in a fog when things move about slowly, dark shapes, changeable.

"The big boys cornered a crow, injured and afraid, hopping rocks at the sorrow crow. At first, they threw little ones, then bigger, lobbed with glee, and then mean glee, and then just mean. The little crow, hit, hit, hit harder, grows a rotten spot, soft and swelling. Such a sorrow crow cornered in the corner of the alley. The sink fits under my armpits and when you lean forward for water, it lifts you up, up on your toes.

"Water by night-light winks on the white surface, blinks on the faucets you turn off, on, off, on, splash a little, little more, and water winking everywhere, and it goes down your pajama top, cold. Maybe I ache, and maybe not, because maybe usually means no. It is not enough ache for a band-aid; it's just a dull feeling up under your ribs, where it doesn't show, under your undershirt in your caged, bleating lamb's heart.

"Unfold black licorice whips at the winking sink in your new shoes, oh little sorrow crow. Brimful and tilting, you carry a rotten spot, and you can't say anything about this maybe-ache."

He put the coin down.

Ben went to the upper 'vista view' deck before lunch. The rush of the train made everything far away appear to turn slowly; houses did this, boats did this. When the train passed trees nearby, they spun in circles, repeating pirouettes until he felt a little dizzy. It reminded him of car rides, lying down in the back seat with his brother (no seatbelts required then), watching the telephone wires loop past, their sturdy brown poles twirling like ballet dancers.

Martin would twist or turn, taking up too much room until Ben shoved him to the outer edge of the back seat and then over it, and the parents intervened. Yes, there were times when he, too, had been mean as a child.

At lunch the dining car was crowded. Tommy spotted a small boy at a table putting a cardboard train together from a template. For a moment, he wondered if he could get one, too. They ordered sandwiches and drinks to take back to their private car, not wishing to risk the virus still circulating. It had begun to rain, a sure sign that they were nearing the coast.

Tommy wondered if they should be wearing masks in common areas of the train. He was tempted to check his phone, see the latest Covid figures in New York, but he didn't. He relished his thin sliced beef piled up on rye and his single pickle, before asking if anyone didn't want their pickle. He got three more this way and sucked them noisily, the others laughing.

He put the penny out on the table.

Sarah picked it up, chose the card, and laughed at the image.

"These days I spend as much time as I can with my new grandson, who is now almost two years old. Yes, James got married! Atticus, he named his son Atticus. I went to visit them in Connecticut.

"Atticus has a little stuffed owl; actually, it's a facsimile of a great horned owl, a fairly dangerous creature, but this one is plush, soft, harmless. On a recent visit, I brought along a book that my children once loved: *Owls in the Family* by Farley Mowat. The book is for older kids and I don't know how much of it he even understood.

"One owl is 'Weeps' and another is 'Wol.' Atticus now thinks he belongs to a family of owls, changing the book title to suit his idea. I went to the bathroom one night, and going through the hallway, I heard him talking. I peered into his room and he was reading the owl book. Well, pretending to read. I noticed that he turned each page carefully, repeating the owl names.

"The rest he just made up! I stood quietly there at the threshold of his room for a long time. I love spending time with him because there is nothing I need to do as his grandmother, nothing but wait for what unfolds from him; that is all."

She put the coin down.

Nora picked it up and frowned. "I have no idea what your word was, Sarah, so I am going to go with nothing!

"Mathematicians and scientists have made much ado about nothing for a long time. Nothing is at the heart of everything, yes, even human beings who make so much of ourselves as if we are something. Bear with me now. I am pretty sure that you know astronomers discovered in 1998 that the universe was expanding; space is increasing over time because there's a gravitational pull of each galaxy on the other galaxies.

"That was supposed to slow down and save everything. But once we discovered 'dark energy,' an unseen energy, we realized it creates a gravitational push. Nothing makes up more than seventy percent of the universe even now. What will be left is nothing. Many find this frightening, but I do not. It is a strange comfort for me to know that love exists amidst nothing, the nothing that we are and will become. Nothing, you could say, is my family of owls, even when I'm with Eugene. I'll say more about him later."

She put the penny down.

Ben smiled, sipped his coffee, and picked it up.

"What can I say? I have learned to love Carl, Carl as Carl, very late in our lives together. Do I love him as your grandson loves his owls? More. He's more than a character in my mind. That, too, but more. He's alive, we're alive. We're all here after this bloody pandemic, even as it goes on."

He put the penny back and Tommy took it up.

Tommy sighed and looked out the window at the wide sky and sea. "What I would give to have a grandchild to read a book about owls with me."

The train went by expanses of the sea and outcroppings of land dense with fir trees, advancing toward winter it seemed, until it stopped at a station in Amherst, Nova Scotia. There was to be a short pause here for some reason. Maybe they were a bit ahead of schedule.

There was a harvest festival or farmers' market set up across from the station. Tommy decided to stretch his legs.

He walked among stacks of pumpkins in a lively outdoor market. People wandered about with things to eat but Tommy wasn't hungry. He looked at the children as they shouted to one another and ran about, returning to adults who were still wearing masks. It was natural for children to run, to wander and return, he realized.

Tommy heard the announcement that the train would leave in ten minutes. He didn't delay joining his friends again.

He found them on the upper berth, waiting for him and his penny. He put it down and Nora reached for it and for the cards.

She considered the letter and chose her word quickly.

"I have wondered about the sheer coincidence of that moment of meeting Eugene in the Phoenix Park in Dublin during a rainstorm almost two years ago. What if it had not rained? Or I had taken a different path? Or had I not stopped for tea? And, was that meeting, and our marriage six months later, already unfolding in our word game?

"I said I had little interest in sex when we met the last time. What did I know? Maybe what I did not know was there in the word game, too. I certainly noticed Eugene! I think of the unlikeliness of that first meeting sometimes as I fall asleep. Sometimes I don't fall asleep at all thinking about it."

She put the coin down and Tommy picked it up.

Tommy crossed his leg, jiggled one foot, and waited for the words to arrive.

"I had to ask myself: Were you asleep when you were thinking about those distracting details? They are still my nemesis! I am drawn to things that compel my attention and displace the present moment. No, the things *become* the present. During the pandemic, we lived through these odd details, at least to some extent: think of the vividness of bird songs alone!

"Sounds stay with me: the shouted conversation of a child sitting on one curb of an empty street, her friend on the opposite curb, their mothers hovering nearby with cups of coffee, softer voices. I open the window a crack to hear better, to assure myself that these are real voices. What are they saying in those high-pitched kids' tones? I thought I'd feel less alone; I was very much alone.

"Each one of us lives with the solitary experience of hours like that. Words move between us in the silent beats of air. Quite often, I don't follow. As an analyst, people think I know something and can solve things, but their words go through me, as if I'm a magnet, or a messenger—these are words I must pass back to the speaker.

"Sometimes their words stun me, as if the sounds are the barbs, stings of a rich insect life that goes on and on. Outside, the world goes on; inside, such richness, such loneliness!"

Ben looked at Tommy still holding the penny and thought of what strange things the pandemic had imposed on them all and left them with, for good and for ill.

Tommy put the coin down and Ben took it up.

"There was a point when I thought I might have to go to a hospital," Ben began. "Carl and I had packed our individual 'go bags' for this very eventuality. It was an unthinkable loneliness to be apart and yet we prepared. We had all our crucial papers, toothbrushes, pajamas, even books, and certainly extra phone cords.

"I was using a pulse oximeter, seeing my oxygen uptake go down, and I was so freighted, frighted, yes, I mean freighted with fright! I was struggling and exhausted, and I really thought that I should go to Cooley Dickinson, our local hospital. But I could not leave him. Such richness, I could not leave Carl and leave my life. So, I risked everything to stay at home with him."

Hearing himself say this, Ben knew it was true. He put the coin down and Sarah took it.

Sarah held the penny; it was warm. Could she speak about this? If not here, where?

"Jenny's a nurse. I'm not sure I said that before. She left for work while we stayed at home; she left us every day. For a time, she worked shifts during the week, but then she took a weekend shift on a Covid ward. On Sunday night she'd leave her outer clothes in the garage and shout that she was back at home, so we could all avoid her. She'd shower, antigen test, and emerge in a mask.

"We were, all of us, freighted with fright, what a perfect phrase! Even though we tried to ignore it and just carry on.

"I remember seeing that someone had picked the last of the tomatoes I was growing on the back deck in pots all summer long into September. It was Jenny who had brought them into the kitchen and lined them up on all the windowsills, still green. I was furious that she picked them without my permission, furious that she risked her life every day without my permission.

"I was looking out the kitchen window on a wet day, watching the way rain falls as a mist. I had to move my body, so I started cleaning the house. It was one of the things I did a lot in 2021.

"On this day I seek out Mr. Kleen, spelled with a K, his robust arms and white t-shirt stretched across his chest. Windex next, aqua-blue, like the sky, that beautiful blue you squirt on glass. Ovens are the worst. Brown water drips down your sleeve as you clean the oven ceiling. The baking racks mark your favorite blue jeans.

"When I finished the oven, I saw that grease had spattered the stovetop where Tyler had been frying up chips for dinner the previous night. I was on a diet and didn't eat them. Why am *I* cleaning the stovetop? Tyler was doing school up in her room, or rather anything but school. I call up the stairs for her to come down.

"I go up to her room and see that she is curled up on her bed and struggling to breathe. I call out to Jack to call 911. I say, 'Don't die, Tyler; don't you dare die.' No one could accompany her to the hospital that day. She did not go to the same hospital where Jenny worked, but to a pediatric ward in a hospital closer to us. Tyler was there for a week. I had resented her, not knowing how to manage or help with her schoolwork. I didn't want to hear anything about her experience or struggle.

"And Jenny? To me, she was still a child herself, and I was the righteous, frightened mother who thought her daughter was careless, and whom she, in turn, ignored. But some nurse stayed with Tyler when we could not, some nurse saw her through the worst of it. There was a nurse's voice on the phone for us when we knew nothing."

Sarah stopped there and put the penny on the table.

She looked out of the window, saw clouds in motion with the movement of the train, little windows of clouds changing, changing.

Nora counted nine houses, four horses, twenty-three painted signs, one man standing in a boat by a pier.

Ben noticed they had entered Truro, and for a moment, felt he was on Cape Cod again as a small boy with his grandparents. The sea and light brought their voices back to him, not their faces, just their voices.

Twenty-three hours had flown. They had spent more time in silence than ever before or with anyone else. The silences were long and comfortable, rich with the echo of their words, with their gestures and glances. They had played the word game intensely again and wondered at what they managed to say and all that was still unsayable.

Entering Halifax, the train tracks widened and crossed with other tracks and routes. Billboards, cranes, and silos along the tracks loomed up as their train moved toward the station. Screeching and mewling, the train slowed, shedding luminosities if not actual sparks.

The sudden shadow of the station roof signaled their entry into a space carved up with platforms and cement columns.

Ben closed his eyes before he stood to leave, as though he could stop time in stillness, as a tightrope walker must still himself before taking the next step.

Epilogue

To make a little Epilogue and briefe collection of what thou deliveredst.
—Hawkins, 1646, *Oxford English Dictionary*

That was the last word game. Or was it?

The four friends went to dinner in Halifax and stayed the night in a hotel. Meeting the next day in the Fairview Lawn Cemetery, they went to see the graves of victims of the Titanic and stood together at the *grave of the unknown child*.

It was there that they made a commitment to continue to meet and play the word game.

Every three years, they took train journeys all around the world. Tyler joined them in their next French-Swiss journey. Atticus, eager to take part, came along on a journey from London to Brussels when he was eleven years old.

With the two young people, they traveled into puzzlement, contradiction, paradox, enigma. Into memory, forgetting, revisions, a palimpsest of words and afterwords. Doors opened the unmarked territories of their voices. They laughed a lot, much more than during the first train journeys. Words snagged at them between journeys. Silences surrounded them.

The memories of earlier word games and their echoes became part of future journeys. How they laughed to remember Nora's 'I can't claim sex was ever a very intense interest. No, I mean that.'

"Something about outposts, wasn't it?"

"No, that was mine," Sarah chirped up.

The children broke some rules and made new rules. Questions were allowed, but one did not need to answer. Nor was it possible sometimes. Nora, who loved explanations, welcomed questions. Atticus had many. Ben hardly ever addressed any question directly. Asked about Carl, he simply said, "For a long time, I went to bed early."

Recognizing Proust, Sarah chuckled. Atticus squinted through his glasses and wondered why this was funny.

On a train from Edinburgh to London two complete strangers in their twenties, traveling together as friends, joined them after overhearing the strange and intense word game, and stayed for life. They insisted on talking about democracy and climate change, and everyone agreed.

When Tommy died, they nearly quit.

Then they remembered: 'The cat, entirely dislodged now, shakes itself and turns to lick off the last of the ketchup...a tongue cleaving through fur, a cat-a-comb.' They saw that only *they* could keep Tommy as part of them, part of the word game, in this way.

"Would you please pass me the cats-up?" Atticus piped up. They all laughed.

"Hey, didn't Tommy have a cat named Freud?" Tyler added.

It would seem there could be no end.

I want to thank Zoe Thirku for conversations over cups of tea and encouraging me to continue working on this novel.

Some of the monologues in this book originated in the Lismore Railway Station Writers group, which I led for five summers in the early 2000s. Writing in the long Irish summer evenings in good company was a gift of time and experimentation. I am indebted to each of you.

I am grateful to Íde B. O'Carroll, my beloved wife, and Mary M. Rogers, my sister, as my first readers who read many renditions, including the last one.

I wish to acknowledge the GIFRIC analysts who inspired earlier versions of this work: Willy Apollon, Danielle Bergeron, and Lucie Cantin.

I am grateful to my readers of the completed book for their generous gifts of time, honesty, and enthusiasm: Elizabeth Silver, Anne Downes, Suzi Naiburg, Aida Keane, Jonathan Lash, and Pauline O'Callaghan.

Thank you, Jonathan Lash, for referring me to Austin Macauley Publishers, and to everyone on the production team.

Advanced Praise

A deck of bespoke playing cards, used in an invented word game, is central in this deeply poetic novel. Rogers' skillful etchings, lithographs, monoprints and paintings grace the cards. These images, ranging from delicately depicted animals to mysterious portals, can't help but serve as evocative catalysts for the characters' story telling. At first disconcerting (since they are not the traditional symbols on playing cards) they challenge our assumptions, shift our perceptions, and invite the reader into a world of imagination and dreams, where anything is possible.

—Liz Chalfin, Artist Printmaker, and Founder of *Zea Mays Printmaking*, Florence, MA

What happens when one of the most talented psychoanalysts today decides to write a novel? Something very special indeed. *After Words* is a book for everyone interested in the intricacies of the human condition rendered with extraordinary everydayness and a deeply moving layering of human interaction, friendship, and storytelling. Drawing from the psychoanalyst's art of listening for the truth beyond the tried and told, Annie Rogers crafts an epic story that is beautifully compelling and tests all the reader's senses and emotions. Words can heal but in doing so open up wounds. Love can make the unbearable bearable. In our near post-Covid world, this book is a monument to the necessity of making stories, finding words, mourning loss, and sharing our humanity with each other.

—Eve Watson, Psychoanalyst, Dublin, Ireland, author of *Clinical Encounters in Sexuality: Psychoanalytic Practice and Queer Theory*

I didn't want *After Words* to end--I wanted to continue to spend time in the presence of the engaging, smart, and lyrical writing, the appealing characters, their insightful conversations. In these pages Rogers captures the richness, the complexity, the at once-realness and dreamlike qualities of human experience. I've long admired Annie Rogers' nonfiction, which brings together deep empathy and brilliant insights into the nature of language, suffering and healing. It's exciting to see Rogers' debut novel. It was a great pleasure to read; I wish there were more books like it!

—Nadia Colburn, author of *I Say the Sky*

Made in United States
North Haven, CT
09 December 2024